Receive a free short story set in the HARD PLACE world when you sign up for
the HARD PLACE newsletter.
https://www.deadcatstud.io/

A SINGLE ROUND

**A COLLECTION OF STORIES
FROM A HARD PLACE
BY R A JACOBSON**

deadcatstudio

R A JACOBSON

A Single Round
© 2020, R A Jacobson
Published by Deadcat Studio
illustrations by Rick Jacobson

rajacobson@deadcatstud.io

Tune every Thursday to the "A Single Round" podcast wherever you listen to your podcasts or go to Deadcatstud.io to listen.
While you are there, check out the merchandise.
Whether it's a t-shirt, a mug or a phone case, we got you covered.

If you are enjoying the world that Jacob and the other characters live in,
'HARD PLACE,' the novel will be released next year.
Sign up to be notified of the released date as well as the release date of the graphic novel currently in the works.

Join our mailing list at Deadcatstud.io

All rights reserved. Printed in the United States of America. No part of this book may be used or reproduced in any manner whatsoever without written permission except in the case of brief quotations embodied in critical articles or reviews.

This book is a work of fiction. Names, characters, businesses, organizations, places, events and incidents either are the product of the author's imagination or are used fictitiously. Any resemblance to actual persons, living or dead, events, or locales is entirely coincidental.

Book and Cover design by Deadcat Studio
Text set in Bookman Old Style
ISBN: 978-1-7773086-5-0

First Edition: October 2020

10 9 8 7 6 5 4 3 2 1

A SINGLE ROUND

CONTENTS

JOHNNY FUCKING CARSON	1
TOGETHER FOREVER	15
BECOMING FAMOUS	47
REDWING	57
DOC's CHOICE	65
THE GROUNDED	83
THE DOGWALKER	109
Alison says yes	110
Alfredo disappears	113
Alison doesn't stoop and scoop	121
Alfredo has a plan	124
Misty has a bite	131
The Plan	133
A coffee?	138
The first job	139
The man in the park	141
THE RIDE	145

R A JACOBSON

...then with a hop and a swift peck, the crow had the head's right eye.

A SINGLE ROUND

CHAPTER 1

JOHNNY FUCKING CARSON

The head sat upright, staring down the dotted line of Highway 11, looking south. The white line reflected in the unmoving, unblinking eyes. The head had been severed cleanly somewhere else. There was almost no blood around it on the pavement. The face had a look of resignation as if being here without a body was inevitable.

It wasn't clear if it had been placed in that spot or if it had been thrown and simply landed there. It had been there since late in the evening, well past dark.

It had sat there through the night watching the stars roll overhead. A few curious animals had come to check on it, but none had disturbed it. One more adventurous squirrel had taken a small bite out of the head's left ear, but nothing more. No coyotes or wolves had come by to take it off for a meal. And so it sat, watching the night pass.

Several cars had flown past, barely missing it. None had noticed, or at least none had stopped. Just bright headlights blaring in its eyes, then as the car passed, a roar and rush of wind or a distant sound behind the head, of an oncoming vehicle then a roar and a rush of wind and taillights disappearing down the road in front.

Once a semi festooned with orange lights appeared in the distance. Its glaring headlights could be seen far down the road, even from this low angle.

The driver was wandering a bit, maybe tired, just not paying attention. The semi came closer, closer than any other vehicle, or perhaps that's just how it felt. It felt like the semi was going to flatten the head into messy mush, but it screamed past, the huge wind rocking it even though the dried blood had glued the head to the road.

It was quiet for a long while. The sky went black as the stars disappeared behind a roving bank of clouds. When they passed, the sky was already lightening. On its left, a thin line of pink announced morning. Slowly, pink turned orange, then yellow, and the sun burst over the trees. The head cast a long bluish shadow across the pavement.

With the sun came the flies, buzzing around. It wasn't long before a crow landed next to the head. It paced back and forth, talking to itself.

"Well, dis is a fine ting. Some goods eats der, but it's a strange ting too. Might be one of dem trappy things. Yeser jus might. Never know what's gonna gitcha. "It strutted around, hopping every few steps, getting a bit closer with each hop.

"Yeser some good eats. Dem eyeballies are soo tasty special iffin day ain't all dried up. Deez be lookin far fresh. Yesser. "With a hop and a swift peck, the crow had the head's right eye.

The crow tossed its head back, swallowed the eyeball whole, and cawed. It hopped around, doing a sort of dance.

A SINGLE ROUND

"Yumm da yumm da yummity,"it croaked.

Tipping its head on its side, it looked at the face in front of it. It hopped forward, aiming to snatch for the other eye.

The quiet was torn by the unmistakable sound of a motorbike gearing down. The crow looked at the head's delicious remaining eye, cawed, and with a flap of its wings, pulled into the air.

The bike glided to a stop on the shoulder of the road. It rumbled loudly once, then quieted. Leather creaked as the rider kicked the stand out. With hands on his lower back, he stood and arched his spine. A small groan escaped.

Jacob was a tall man over 6 feet, broad-shouldered, well into his forties, and a face half-covered with a long greying beard. He wore denim over his heavy snoot boots, a black t-shirt and his leather jacket. Over his jacket, he had a denim vest with a patch on the back. Turning the peak of his cap forward, Jacob pulled off his shades and looked at the head on the road.

"Here's Johnny. "He laughed lightly. "Well, you've looked better. So, are you dead dead or are you just dead? "
Jacob sat back on his bike and crossed his boots.
After a minute, the remaining eye in the head rolled dryly and looked toward Jacob.

"So, not dead. "He said. "Do you still have your vocal cords? It would make things easier to find out what killed you. "
A sound like someone trying to clear an extremely dry throat came from the head, and it said. "How can you hear me? "

Jacob chuckled, "I'm marked. "

"Oh ya, you're the idiot that sold his soul for a truck. A fucking truck! "

"That's not the complete story, "Jacob said and scowled. He had heard that his entire life, and he was tired of it.

"A truck! "The head made a sound that might have been a laugh or a cough.

Across from Jacob, the crow cawed, "Hungry! be going, tall walker. Be off. "

Jacob scowl deepened as he looked up at the crow. He liked ravens. They were smart and disdainful, maybe a bit arrogant, but they at least would respond with a reasonable answer. But crows, he hated crows. Crows were intelligent but spiteful and cruel, not to mention one had betrayed him a while back.

"Fuck off, "Jacob said.

The head's one eye rolled awkwardly over to look at the crow pacing hungrily at the edge of the pavement. The eye rolled back toward Jacob.

"Kill it, "the head gravelled.

Jacob looked at the head and back at the crow. He was tempted, but he knew crows were messengers and gossips. It would come back on him. He growled. From inside his coat, he pulled out his gun. It was a Ruger 480. It was too big and made too much noise, but when it came out, people noticed, which sometimes was all you needed. He looked down his nose at the crow and raised the heavy gun. The head's one eye rolled to look. The crow stopped pacing.

"Not gonna. Not gonna. No sirree. Not gonna. "With a long squawk, it jumped into the air and flew off. Jacob half grinned and put the Ruger back in his leathers. The head's single eye followed the crow as it rose and headed south, joined by several other black shapes.

"You didn't kill it! Why didn't you kill it? It took my eye! "

"Ya, not my problem. Who cut off yer head, that's what I'm interested in. "

Jacob smiled as he enjoyed watching the face attempt a scowl.

"I don't remember, "the head said, sounding put-out.

"Now now, Johnny. I'm just here to help, "Jacob said, still smiling.

"So, you know who I am? "The head sort of smiled. Jacob knew the man whose head this was. He hadn't had any dealings with him but knew him by reputation. He was known as one of the more slimier car dealers around selling P.O.S. to anyone and everyone.

He was known to be marked, but what he had sold his soul

A SINGLE ROUND

for Jacob wasn't sure. He wasn't particularly rich or good looking, nor was he all that successful. Perhaps he asked the Judge to be more of a slime bucket than he already had been, but Jacob thought that wasn't likely.

He was named by cruel parents, John Carson. It must've been hell growing up with that name, but he made it a joke on his T.V. commercials for his dealership. "Here's Johnny "had become his slogan.

Jacob looked across the fields. A murder of crows was circling, making a distant racket. He looked back to the head.

"Look, you want my help or not? "

"Help! How the fuck can you help? Are you going to find my body? Put me back together? "

"Well, no, can't rightly do that, but," he paused. "I could at least get the thing that got you. "

"What are you, the poleece? Gonna make the Judge pay? I heard how that went. "Again, the head struggled to chuckle.
Jacob looked down the road.

"Naw nuthin like that. Jus tryin' to figure it. Need ta know what got ya, is all. "He said.

The head's remaining eye turned away from Jacob to look down the road. A car was coming, the sun glinting off its roof. Jacob heard it and looked.

"Now what do you suppose, that's maybe one of the marked coming to put an end to our little conversation? "

The car was coming fast. Its engine howled as it accelerated.

"Yup, I bet our friendly crow spoke to someone, and they spoke to someone else who doesn't want me to find out who done you. "

The head's remaining eye widened, then turned.

"It was a fucking wolf. How the fuck could I know who it was! Now move me! "

Jacob uncrossed his boots and stood.

"A wolf? What colour was its fur? "

"Grey, I think with black. "

The car was close now. Jacob knew it. It belonged to Frank, the owner of the Ol' Scratch Tavern. A beat down 93 Capri, a real P.O.S. The man had no taste. He'd probably bought it from Johnny here. The world is not without irony.

Jacob enjoyed going to the Ol' Scratch usually went on Wednesday, for live music and Thursday, for wings. He conceded that Frank had good taste in music if nothing else.

Jacob straddled the bike, heard the head curse, then a wet thump. A roar of an overstrained engine. Frank and his P.O.S. sped away.

Jacob put his sunglasses back on, kicked the bike into life and looked where the head had been. It wasn't there anymore. Bits of bone, grey mush and gore were splattered across the pavement. A crow landed among the mess.

"So sad. Was tasty bits. Was juicy. Still good yesir yesir "it hopped about picking up bits and tossing them back.

Jacob pulled out onto the highway and rumbled down the pavement.

A single light bulb hung from the ceiling and glinted off the dishes and pots in the sink. It lit the small kitchen with an uncertain light that cast indistinct shadows on the scuffed linoleum floor.

The man at the table was dirty. He was dressed in jeans and black T-shirt. Both were faded and old. The knees of his jeans were torn, and he wore heavy boots caked with mud. Over the back of his chair hung a well-worn black leather jacket, a denim vest over it with a patch on the back.

He was slim to the point of skinny. He slouched in his chair; legs spread under the table. He had a thin, pale face with a patchy beard around a cruel mouth set in a tight, hard line.

His eyes, heavy-lidded, hard and dark, under his shaggy

eyebrows burned with a strange heat. They were ringed with dark shadows as if he hadn't slept in days. The brow under his long lank black hair was furrowed. He stared straight ahead.

He was waiting.

Both arms rested on the table in front of him. His left hand loosely touched a glass half full of amber whiskey. An empty bottle of 'Jack' stood testament. His right rested near a gun, a Glock 19. It was loaded.

He knew that if you put a gun on the table in a meeting such as he was waiting for, you couldn't take it off. It was there. It was a statement. It was a declaration, and there was no going back from that.

He stared at his glass and oddly noticed the table. It was a chrome table with a mica top. It had been here for as long as he could remember.

His mother had bought it before he was born. He had had his first solid food at it. He had eaten cereal, what homework he had done, he had done here, and here he'd screamed at his father.' It was in the heart of the house,' his mother had been fond of saying. It had been a bright, cheerful yellow, he supposed. Now it was a dull, muddy, indistinct colour. This is where he ate and drank, sometimes with his friends playing cards but more often alone. He even rebuilt a carburetor for his Harley on it.

Now both his bastard father and his mother were long dead. He sat at the table, waiting to kill or be killed. He wasn't sure which outcome he wanted.

Outside distantly, he heard the unmistakable sound of a loud knucklehead on the road gearing down as it slowed for his drive. That would be Jacob. He'd recognize that bike's sound anywhere. Many years ago, he'd helped put it together, and he still loved it.

The bike rolled closer, then it was right outside the house. After a pause, he heard it shut down, and a minute after that, there was a knock at his door.

"Ya, "he called, and Jacob pushed open the door.

Jacob stepped in, looked at him, saw the gun, ignored it, looked at the empty bottle of Jack and smiled.

"Hey Pete, drinking legit?" Jacob asked.

"Ya." Pete looked at the bottle. "It's been sitting in the cupboard since my pa passed. It was the only thing he left. A half-full bottle of his favourite friend."

Jacob stepped forward and pulled out a chair. Sat down, his leather jacket creaking.

"Sometimes, it's the only friend you kin find." Pete mused. He grunted, staring at the glass in his hand. He knocked it back.

"I'd offer ya sum, but I'm all out."

Jacob smiled. "S'pose you know why I'm here?"

"Ya, I s'pose I do." He held the empty glass up, looked at it for a second, he set it down and looked up at Jacob. "You ever wish you hadn't made yer deal?"

Jacob scowled. "Every fucking day! All day long!"

Pete looked back down at his empty glass.

"I never had until yesterday. Ya it wasn't what I thought, but it's better than no deal. Any deal is better than no deal, right?"

Jacob's scowl deepened.

"I mean, if I dint have the deal I won't be anybody. Just another fucking loser ahwta work."

"You were hot shit in high school. A football star. Got all the cheerleaders." Jacob said.

With a wry smile, Pete said, "Ya, that was the deal."

"The deal? What did you git marked for?" Jacob asked.

"It's fucking embarrassing. I was a big reader in Grade 10. I thought it was cool to be as fast and as strong as a wolf. I'd read it in some book." Pete looked at the empty glass in front of him.

"Well, you can't say The Judge doesn't have a sense of humour," Jacob said.

"Really fucking funny.' Bout a month after school started, I was riding high. The girls were all over me. Made the football team. Looked like I'd be the quarterback. I got into a fight. Nearly killed the kid. It got all hushed up. I was' important' to the team, and Coach said he needed me, so it was put down to kids being kids. I know the kid's dad was fucking pissed. Wanted to go to the cops, but nothing happened. "Pete fingered his empty glass.

He stood and walked to the cupboard over the sink. He pulled down a glass bleach bottle. He undid the cap with his back to Jacob, tipped the bottle back, and took a swallow. He set the bottle down and leaned on the sink, his head lowered.

"A couple nights later was the full fucking moon. And you know what happened. I woke the next morning, miles from the farm, nearly naked. I ran the whole way back. Made it without anyone seeing me. "He said. He picked up the beach bottle, walked back to the table, and offered the bottle to Jacob. Jacob took it.

"This one of mine? "Jacob asked.

"Ya, last September, I think. Had it a while. It was a good batch. Some of your shine can get a might strong. "

Jacob looked at Pete, then at the bottle.

"Getting damn hard to find glass bottles like this anymore. "He took a swallow. Grunted, "That's pretty smooth, even if I say so myself. "He half-smiled.

Pete sat down, took the bottle back and took a deep pull on it. He wiped his mouth and set the bottle down.

"The thing is, I felt great, but I didn't have a clue what I had done. Course it wasn't me; it was the demon inside of me coming out to play.' He' did some terrible things. I tried very hard notice. I've learned to control it, and when it feels like it's gonna be bad, I got a room in the cellar that has a lock on a timer. "

Jacob reached and took the bottle, took a swallow, set it down and gave it a flick. It slid a few inches across the table toward Pete.

"Ya see, that fucker I beat up never forgot. He never let it go. After high school, it got worse. Took every chance he could to cause me grief. Called the cops on me every fucking week felt like. Then he made his deal. And things got real interestin'. "

Pete slid his chair back and stood. Starting to pace. After a couple turns around the kitchen, he sat again.

"The cops were always down my throat. Couldn't figure it. Seemed like I'd step out the door, and they'd be waiting. Turns out, they were. He had sold for control of the cops here's about. Didn't even think that were possible, but I guess The Judge's got his ways."

Pete looked at Jacob. There was pain in his eyes.

"He turned hard, turned mean, and it's my fault. What happened is on me. I beat that kid so bad he never was right. It poisoned him."

"Wait. Who we talkin' bout?"Jacob asked.

"Johnny Fucking Carson. Every time I saw one of his fucking commercials, I would nearly smash the T.V."

Jacob grunted, reaching for the bottle.

"Turned out, he wasn't jus fucking with me. He had a sort of a list in his head,"Pete continued. "A list of folk who he felt done him wrong. He used the cops like his own attack dogs. Good folk that were just stupid kids doin stupid kid's shit, but now he was ruining people. Ruining their lives."

Pete leaned forward, "but he turned back to me. He seemed to get tired of just sending cops after me. He wanted to hurt me, and his deal made it sose he wouldn't get caught."

"He went looking for some way to hurt me. He found my daughter. She was just a girl. I don't get to see her so often. He made sure ah that, but…"he paused and looked at his hands in front of him. His grey eyes got moist. "She's just little. Jus had her 16th birthday. I couldn't go to her party. Not supposed to see her without consent, and my ex likes to hold back on that."

"That fucker got me good. Even my ex believed I was dealing meth. I couldn't explain where I went every month for a few days. She's not marked, so it's not a conversation we had."

"That was horrible, but he did sumpin worst. He took her! Jacob, what was I s'pose to do? The fucker had my little girl!"

"I got arrested again. Bogus charge, but I was put in jail for a

A SINGLE ROUND

couple of days. When I got out she was gone. She's missing. He killed her. I know he did. "

"The moon was coming, so I just waited. Figured I'd let the demon deal with him. Just let it loose. Never thought how wrong it would go. Didn't care. Just wanted him dead. "

He paused, looked down at his hands. They shook slightly. He reached for the bottle, looked at it, didn't drink, then set it down.

"Jacob, why are you here? "

"Well, Pete, Clyde suggested I get over here. Ya see, he's got information that you an I don't. Bein' a demon himself an all. "

"Clyde? Oh ya, yer truck. I used to laugh at you. Sold yer soul for a truck. Now it doesn't sound so dumb. "

Jacob smiled. Wasn't the first time he'd heard that.

"Clyde says it wasn't John that took yer kid. "

Pete stood up, knocking his chair back, fists on the table.

"It was him! That fucker did it! He's been after me forever! "

"Semmer down, Pete. It wasn't him. Ya, he's been a real bastard to you, but it wasn't him this time. "

"Bullshit! I smelled her scent over at his house when I went over. My wolf side gives me a bunch of things, an' one of them is real good smell. I stood outside his place before the moon came up, and I could smell her. "

"Ya, I'm sure ya could, but he didn't take her. Pete, this ain't easy ta tell you. She's been seein' John's son, David. You don't see her much an I don't s'pose she'd told you anyhow. Special since she knew yer history an all. "

"I don't believe you, "Pete said, but his voice had a hint of doubt. He picked up his chair and sat, hands flat on the table.

"See, they were having a party. It was David's birthday. The whole family was there, including his young girlfriend. She had run away from your ex to be with David. "

"No, "Pete said.

Jacob sat back. Not sure how to continue.

"How much do you remember when the demon takes over? "

"Of that night, not a lot. It was a strong one. I don't watch the news after the moon run. It's better. "
Jacob sighed.
"The demon killed everyone at the party. Everyone. Tore them to shreds. "Jacob paused, not wanting to say it. Not wanting to be the one to tell him.
Pete stared at him, his eyes growing wide as realization slipped in, unwanted.
"No. "Pete stared at Jacob. "No "
"It was the demon. It wasn't you. It was the demon. It's not your fault. "Jacob said.
Pete fell back in his seat. His eyes wide.
"She wasn't there. No, she couldn't have been. No. Please, no. "
Jacob didn't answer. What could he say?
"Jacob, she wasn't there! She can't. No! "Pete's voice rose. "NO! "
"I'm sorry, Pete, "Jacob mumbled.
They sat looking at each other for a long time, passing the bottle back and forth. They didn't speak.
After a time, Jacob stood. Pete didn't look up. Jacob dug in his pocket and pulled out a bullet. It was a 9 mm.
It would fit in Pete's Glock. He had loaded it himself. He had cast the slug in pure silver.
Jacob looked at the bullet, turned, walked out of the little house, and down the steps to his bike. He pulled his denim vest out of the saddlebag where he stored it before entering the house, and put it back on.
He straddled his bike. For a minute, he sat listening, hearing the night. It was quiet. The darkness was broken by the yellow light spilling from the kitchen window. Far off, a dog barked.
He rose and kicked the bike to life. It rumbled beneath him. He pulled away from the house. He was just turning on to the road when he heard a loud crack. Might have been a backfire.

A SINGLE ROUND

Soo tall walker, R you likin whatcha reedin?
Its fehr good stuf. Yes sir yes sir.
Iffin dat bein whacha thinin. Hop o'er ta the place fer books and tings and be leaven one ah dem whatcha call a 'rear view?"

PECK HERE!

R A JACOBSON

...they sat around looking at the fire.

A SINGLE ROUND

CHAPTER 2

TOGETHER FOREVER

The day she died was the happiest of his life.

    The trip had been the talk for months. It was June 1st. It was a Friday, and they skipped afternoon class and were heading to Stoney lake. It had all been planned.
    Jason was going to drive his truck. Cooper, Mary Ann, Tommy were going to ride with him. Alice, George and Leslie were going to ride in Dean's beat down white Mustang. Kirk, Tyler and Kirk's cousin were coming in Kirk's mom's car, maybe. Tommy kinda doubted it. Kirk had gotten in trouble the weekend before. His parents weren't really in the lending mood and would be even less so

when they saw Kirk's report card. But Tommy hoped it would work out. After all, Kirk was bringing some weed, and that would just make it all so much cooler.

"Is that fucker Kirk coming?" Jason yelled as they stepped out to the parking lot of the school. He could be such an ass.
"Don't know. I think so," Tommy replied, not really wanting to talk about it.
The parking lot was already half empty, even the teacher's side was looking sparse. Many people were already off to enjoy their long weekend.

Tommy loped over to Jason's truck and pulled himself up on the hood.

Jason's truck was a newish Silverado two-tone, a light brown, he called it 'baby shit brown' and white. He had put a set of slot mags and serious boots on the back. It looked cool.

Tommy was envious, but Jason's dad owned a Ford dealership that took a lot of used cars in on trade. Jason was lucky. His dad had got him this truck for a song. Jason worked for his dad, washing cars and running errands to pay for gas and beer. He didn't talk about his dad much. When he did, Tommy sensed Jason didn't like his dad. He often joked about his dad's name, Johnny Carson. Carson Ford was the biggest dealership in the area. They had TV commercials with the catchphrase `Here's Johnny.' Tommy wondered why he didn't get sued for using that line, but it was his name, so maybe that was OK.

Tommy slid off the hood of the truck when he saw Cooper and Mary Ann pushing out the school doors, laughing about something. Tommy liked Cooper. She was cute and always laughed at his jokes. He smiled. This weekend was going to be fun.

Cooper and Mary Ann walked up to Jason's truck, still smiling.
"Well. Let's get going." Tommy said, opening the door for Cooper. Cooper looked back at Mary Ann and giggled. Tommy blushed.

Mary Ann and Jason had been dating for nearly a month now. She walked around the hood of the truck, kissed Jason and climbed

A SINGLE ROUND

in. Jason followed. Tommy and Jason closed the door at nearly the same moment.

Jason smiled as he revved the engine and listened to its rumble. He looked over to Tommy. Tommy smiled back, also enjoying the sound.

"So all your stuff is over at Mary Ann's?" Tommy asked, interrupting the girls' huddled conversation. They turned and looked at him.

"Yes," Mary Ann answered and with a disdainful shake of her head. They resumed their conversation.

Tommy caught Jason's sideways glance and frowned. He looked out the window. Jason stomped on the gas when he turned onto the street. His tires squealed amid the roar of his engine. In spite of himself, Tommy smiled.

Mary Ann lived close to the school. Cooper had slept over at her house the night before, packed and ready for the weekend.

"You gonna bring your guitar?" Jason asked Tommy over the girls' heads. They looked up and turned to him.

"Naw. Thought I'd leave it at home," he said. The girls' turned back to their conversation.

He had been practicing for this weekend all semester and was sure he could probably do a few good tunes by the fire, but at the last moment, he had chickened out. He silently cursed Jason for bringing it up. Jason knew he hadn't brought it. His backpack and his tent were in the back of the truck, and that's it. No guitar.

They sat in silence, the girls chatting between them until they got to Mary Ann's house.

"Back in a sec" Mary Ann kissed Jason on the cheek. Tommy got out, letting them slide past him. He stood holding the door and watched the girls run across the lawn.

"Get in. They'll be a while." Jason shut off the truck. Tommy looked at the house then jumped back into the truck.

"We'll stop at the mall and get food and beer. You got money?" Jason looked at Tommy

"Yes. I have money." Tommy didn't have a job, so he'd

borrowed some cash from his uncle. It was a nice feeling to have something to spend without having to tell his mom what he wanted to buy.

Jason pressed 'play' on his tape deck and leaned back. Led Zeppelin powered out the immigrant song. Tommy smiled. He loved this song. Jason was right. The girls took their time.

"What do you think of Cooper?" Jason asked.

"She's OK," Tommy responded.

"Are you going to make a play for her?"

"I dunno. Why? You think I should."

Jason shrugged. "What do you think of Mary Ann?"

"She's nice." Tommy was surprised. This was far more conversation about girls than he and Jason had had. "Why, what's up?"

Jason seemed to be listening to the music. Then he said, "if you aren't thinking about hitting on Cooper. I thought that I might."

"What about Mary Ann?" Tommy asked.

"She's OK, but I'm bored."

And that was that. Conversation over. Tommy wasn't sure what he could say after that, and Jason had said what he needed to say.

Tommy realized his idea of how this weekend was going to go had just shifted. It suddenly wasn't going to be as much fun as he thought it was. At the very least, when Jason broke with Mary Ann, she would cast a black cloud over the weekend.

Tommy wasn't sure how Jason was going to shift between best friends. Tommy was pretty sure it wasn't going to happen, and probably he and Jason would end up alone around the fire drinking beer.

The girls returned hauling heavy backpacks, laughing. Tommy got out and helped load the packs into the box of the truck and watched as Jason and Mary Ann kissed. He shook his head and smiled at Cooper. Well, it was going to be interesting.

They drove downtown and crossed Main, then turned left

into the mall parking lot. They pulled into a spot beside Dean's rusted Mustang. Jason and Mary Ann were going for beer. Tommy and Cooper headed for food.
Together they walked into the supermarket. Tommy grabbed a shopping cart. Cooper had a list. Tommy glanced at it. Not much, burger and hot dogs, buns, ketchup, mustard, relish, some chips and Twizzlers.

"Twizzlers?" Tommy asked. Cooper looked up and frowned.
"Ya. Jason loves them."
Tommy grunted. He had never seen Jason eating a Twizzler, but he didn't say so.

They walked down the aisles, Tommy tossing things that weren't on the list. Cooper would sigh and take them out. She didn't seem to think he was funny.

They got to the freezer and got the burgers and wieners, then headed for bread.

"Why don't you go get chips," Cooper said, not looking at him.

"Sure," Tommy said, shrugged, turned and left to look for chips. They were on the next aisle. He picked several large family bags, plain, barbecue and sour cream and onion.
He turned the corner to the bread aisle and stopped. Jason and Cooper were standing, talking. They were very close. He watched. Jason leaned forward and kissed her.

"Got the chips?" Mary Ann stepped past Tommy and froze. "What the fuck!" She stormed forward, murder in her eyes. Tommy turned and walked to the cashier. Behind him, he could hear screaming. He paid for the chips and went out to the parking lot.

When he got to the truck. Dean was standing with Alice and Leslie. George was sitting in the Mustang with the radio on. He was rolling a joint. George could roll the best joints, tight and packed. They burned well. Dean laughed

"Is that what yer gonna eat this weekend?"
Tommy looked at his armload of chips.

"No. Jason and the girls are bringing the beer and food."
Dean laughed again. Over Tommy's shoulder, he could see the trio walking toward them.

"Looks like you're going to go hungry," Dean said.

Tommy turned. They were walking toward the truck, walking as far apart as they could. Mary Ann's arms were crossed, and she was scowling.

When they got close, Mary Ann said, "Dean, drive me home." Dean paused until he saw Jason nod.

"Ah...sure," he said, then he turned to Alice and Leslie, "back in a minute." And he grinned his big toothy grin. He helped Mary Ann with her backpack and opened the door for her. Another big grin and they drove off.

Tommy watched them leave then looked at Jason. The shit didn't stick. Tommy didn't know how it always seemed to work out for him. Anything he wanted, no matter how big, it just worked out. He looked at Jason and Cooper now standing close. Tommy shook his head.

Jason and Cooper ran back into the grocery store and grabbed the food. They came back holding hands. Dean returned, smiling.
Tommy looked at his group of friends. It was amazing how fast things shifted around him. In a few minutes, the three of them were heading out of town.
It was just over an hour's drive to the lake. Jason and Cooper chatted, kissed and were generally annoying. Tommy kinda wished Mary Ann was still here. At least then, Jason would be talking to him, and the girls would be giggling in the middle.

Tommy felt like the third wheel that he was. He watched the trees flash by as they roared down the road. He resigned to spend the weekend watching the newly formed couple lock themselves together.
They arrived with the sun still up. They pulled into the campsite and stepped out—the air smelled of pine and freshwater.

A SINGLE ROUND

It wasn't a busy lake, which made it perfect for a celebratory graduation weekend.

Tommy climbed out of the truck and looked around. In the center of the site was a fire pit surrounded by blackened stones, then sand and patches of grass that led to a larger area of flat grass. That's where they would pitch their tents.

Tommy grabbed his pack, sleeping bag and tent and headed to set up. He promised himself he would pitch it and then go for a swim as soon as they arrived. He knew that later he would be in no shape to do either.

Jason and Cooper walked to the water's edge and kissed. No, that doesn't describe the face lock that ensued. It was nearly obscene.

With the tent up, Tommy crawled in and put on his denim shorts. He was going for a swim. With a towel around his neck, he walked self-consciously across the sand to the water's edge. He dropped the towel. And stepped into the water.

Stoney Lake wasn't very popular because it was really shallow for a long way, then dropped off incredibly fast.

Tommy walked the water that never got higher than his knees. He stopped and looked back at the tiny figures on the beach. He turned, and the water suddenly was up to his belly button. Another step and the water would be above his head.

He dove. The water was colder the deeper he went. He opened his eyes. The sand dropped off into blackness. The blackness menaced him. He surfaced and swam back to a point where he could stand. He looked back to the beach.

Tommy swam toward the beach, but suddenly it wasn't deep enough to swim. He stood and began walking, grateful the sun was warm, and the wind was light.

He looked up and saw Dean's Mustang pull into the campsite next to theirs.

On the beach, Tommy towelled off and walked up to the campsite. Jason and Cooper were nowhere to be seen. Tommy waved to Dean and the group he had brought. He headed for his tent. He would change into his dry jeans and go over and have a laugh.

He walked to his tent and stopped. Fuck! Jason and Copper were in there. He groaned. Of course. He turned and walked to the camp next door.

"Where's Jason?" Alice asked. Tommy had always suspected she had a thing for Jason. George and Leslie were off setting up their tent. They had been together since Grade 9 and moved as one unit, quiet and efficient. In some ways, he envied them. So much of the random, unpredictable shifts in the social connections were beyond them. All this jostling was unknown to them. He watched them walk back from their tent hand in hand. Completely at ease.

"Yes," he thought, "that's what I want."

Jason and Cooper walked over smiling. They didn't have the same relaxed air, but Tommy envied them as well. He scowled at Jason as they passed each other. Jason ignored him. Tommy headed for his tent to change.

When he stepped out of his tent, the sun was low. He pulled his jacket over his T-shirt and walked towards the fire that Dean had started. Halfway there, he turned and walked to Jason's truck, grabbed two folding chairs and carried them back to the fire. He unfolded them, and Jason grabbed them and sat handing one to Cooper.

Tommy sighed and turned. He walked back to the truck to get the other two chairs. He was reaching into the box to pick them up when Kirk drove up and parked behind Dean's Mustang.

So, he got his mom's car after all. Tommy wondered if he had told his mom about the report card. He didn't think so. He climbed into the box to reach the chairs then jumped down out of the truck.

He walked toward the fire looking at his friends laughing. Jason and Cooper were leaning toward each other. Their hands continued to touch each other. Tommy wondered how long this would last. How long would it take for Jason to start getting bored?

George and Leslie were sitting together on a blanket on the

A SINGLE ROUND

sand, smiling, looking around at the crowd, enjoying the back and forth.

Kirk was digging through a cooler with Tyler giving him directions. Off to the side and standing beside him was a girl Tommy didn't know. She was slight and delicate, with a bag in her hand and a guitar case on her back. He watched her. She was unknown but somehow not unsure. She stepped to her right, closer to the fire. She was almost entirely silhouetted by the fire. Kirk said something, and she turned her head to look at him, her ponytail flying.

Tommy set the chairs down beside Jason, who didn't notice, then he walked over to Kirk to get a beer.

"Hey, Kirk. toss me a beer." Tommy said.

Kirk, his head still in the cooler, said nothing, just passed a beer back. The unknown girl took it and passed it to Tommy.

"Thanks," he said, but she had turned away to take another beer, then she turned back, beer in hand and Tommy's heart did something he had never felt before. He couldn't have described it if his life depended on it. When she looked up at him, he died and lived completely in a millisecond.

"You're welcome," she grinned and tapped his beer that he had completely forgotten about, with hers and then she took a swallow looking at him.

"I'm Rebecca" she extended her hand.

Tommy looked at her, then said, "Tommy" and grasped the offered hand. She laughed and looked at Kirk,

"I'm Kirk's cousin."

"Ya, I figured." He cursed his lameness.

She smiled and took another sip of beer and looked around.

"You want to sit by the fire?" Tommy asked, unable to think of anything else to say.

"Sure." She looked at Kirk, his head still in the cooler. Tyler had walked off and was talking with Alice. Now Kirk was swearing. Something about Jason forgetting his beer or some such. She shrugged and followed Tommy to the chairs he had set up next to

Jason. Jason looked up as they approached. Tommy scowled at Jason, who grinned back and turned to Cooper.

Rebecca slipped her guitar off her back, placed it behind her chair and sat.

"You play?" Tommy asked, indicating the guitar case. Dumb thing to say. Of course, she played. Again, he cursed his stupidity.

"Ya little. I thought tonight I would try to play in front of strangers instead of just a couple of friends. I nearly left it at home, then Kirk just picked it up and threw it in the car. I was mad for a bit but maybe later when people have some beer in them. We'll see. I'm not very good" she took a sip of beer and looked around at the firelit faces.

"I wish Kirk had been around when I packed for this weekend. I may have had my guitar as well."

"Oh, you play?"

"Only to myself in my room. No one has heard me except my mom and only through a closed door. She says I'm real good, but moms always say shit like that."

Rebecca laughed lightly.
"Maybe you'll play for me," she said and looked at him. Tommy felt his heart stagger.

The sun had set, and the darkness was upon them. Dean had backed his Mustang close to the group, opened the hatchback and had his stereo booming. More Led Zeppelin. It seemed to be the band of the weekend. That was OK with Tommy.

Tommy and Rebecca talked about songs they liked, songs they wanted to learn, songs they knew. It was easy. They talked, and Tommy forgot he was talking to a girl. He was talking to a friend with the comfort and ease he had with any of his friends, but he also was keenly aware of her otherness. The complete girlness of her. He found himself amazed she said things he had thought. Amazed that she had the courage to say out loud thoughts he wouldn't have admitted and also amazed that there was a girl that thought as he did. Maybe girls weren't that different, after all.

At some point, Tommy wasn't sure when George had lit the barbecue

A SINGLE ROUND

and, with Leslie's help, was cooking burgers. Tommy realized he was hungry when the scent of the meat cooking wafted past him.

"Shit, I'm hungry," he blurted. Rebecca chuckled.

"Ya me too." She smiled at him, "Want a burger or a hotdog?" She stood.

Surprised, he said, "a burger would be great." And he smiled.

"Great. Get me one too." She laughed at the fading smile on his face, then stood and left, glancing back.

After a bit, she returned, carrying two burgers on paper plates.

"I didn't know if you wanted ketchup or mustard or what, so I guessed you wanted it all, so that's what you got."

"That's perfect." Pleased, he took the plate from her. She sat, placing the plate on her lap and took a bite.

"It's not bad. I wish there was cheese."

"I think we're lucky we have food at all." He said then he told her about what happened at the mall. Rebecca looked at Jason and Cooper. Jason was devouring his burger. Cooper was watching him with a slight frown, then she got up to get herself a burger.

"Well, that's not going to last," Rebecca said with eyebrows raised. Tommy grunted, his mouth full of food. When he finished, he tossed the plate on the fire.

"I think I want a hotdog as well. Can I get you one?"

"Naw. I'm good but maybe grab a bag of chips." She grinned

He smiled back and walked off to get the food. He talked with George for a bit while he ate his hotdog, then got a bag of chips and a couple more beers. He headed back to his chair and saw Dean sitting in his chair. He and Rebecca were talking. She was laughing.

"Shit." He said quietly to himself. She looked up and gestured for him to come. She said something to Dean, who frowned, got up and left.

Tommy smiled as he sat. He handed the chips to her.

"I got you another beer."

"Thanks." She took the fresh beer and pushed it into the sand beside her chair, then finished the one she was drinking. Over the sand incrusted bottle, she looked at Tommy with smiling eyes.

As she munched on chips, they talked lost in their own world. Sometime later, Kirk called across the fire to Rebecca, "Reb, play something."

She shook her head even as she reached for the guitar. Dean walked over and shut off his stereo. Tommy was suddenly aware of how loud it had been.

It was very quiet. No one was talking, and all eyes were on her. Tommy was surprised at how relaxed she looked as she pulled the guitar into her lap. She turned then strummed a couple of times. She smiled at the faces turned toward her, then she looked at Tommy, smiled and looked down and started.

Tommy listened, not sure what she was playing. It was quiet then her voice broke in. It was clear and bright. She sang, hunched over the guitar, looking down.

She sang 'Here Comes The Sun', and as she sang, her head came up. She straightened, and her voice took on a power that gave Tommy goosebumps. She was really good.

When she finished, they all hooted, clapping loudly, calling for more. She looked down, then through her hair, she looked at Tommy.

"Was that OK?" she asked quietly.

"OK? It was fucking amazing! You're really good!" Her head came up, and she smiled.

"Play something else."

"What do you want me to play? Wait, why don't you do a song?"

He leaned back, "Oh no, not after that. I'm nowhere near as good as you."

"Come on." She coaxed.

"Maybe later," he smiled.

"K but for sure. So what should I play?"

"Whatever you like."

"K," she looked at Tommy and smiled, then she turned and looked down at her guitar. Then she looked up and started a quiet version of 'Landslide.' He wasn't a big fan of Fleetwood Mac, but he

A SINGLE ROUND

loved her version. He watched her play and sing. Her playing was good, but her voice. It was amazing. He got lost in her songs. He watched the flames dance, and suddenly it was quiet, and she was nudging him, the guitar held out to him. He looked up from far away and, without thinking, took the guitar.

"Play," she said with a warm smile, and he did.

He had been practicing a version of "Over the Hills and Far Away." He stumbled.

"Start again," she said, and he did, and he played perfectly.

When he sang, he sang for her and smiled when she sang along.

He played every song he knew and some he had only attempted, then he handed the guitar back to her, and she played with everyone singing along.

At one point, George stood and asked if he could sing a song, and Rebecca handed him the guitar. No one knew he played guitar.

He sang "Rocky Mountain High" with a warm, quiet voice, all the while looking at Leslie. When he finished, he leaned down and kissed her and stood and handed the guitar back over protests and calls for more. He just smiled and shook his head.

Rebecca sang a few more songs repeating a couple of Beatle tunes, then put the guitar away. Dean didn't get up to put the music back on, and they sat around looking at the fire. It became very quiet, and in ones and twos, they left the dying fire to find their tents and go to sleep. They watched Kirk and Alice get up and walk hand in hand to Kirk's tent.

Tommy was hating that the evening was coming to an end. He wasn't drunk like he thought he might. He sat beside Rebecca, and they talked quietly then without warning, she stood.

"I'm tired. I need to sleep." Rebecca said. Tommy stood, ready to say good night when she leaned forward and kissed him. Startled, he didn't immediately kiss her back, then he did. He got lost in her soft lips, the smell of her. She pressed herself against him, and they stood there just kissing. Then she pulled away.

"Where's your tent?" and he walked her there.

In the darkness of the small tent, they bumped around as Tommy unrolled his sleeping bag.

"Tommy."

"Yes?"

"Can I borrow your T-shirt?"

"Umm.. sure." he pulled it over his head and handed it to her.

"I left all my stuff in Kirk's tent, and well, he isn't alone." He could just make out her smile in the light that came through the tent from the light of the fire. She turned her back to him and pulled off her shirt and bra and slipped his T-shirt on, then sat and struggled out of her jeans then deftly slipped into the sleeping bag. Tommy pulled off his jeans and slid in beside. She felt so warm.

"Oh my god, you're freezing!" She rolled her back to him then snuggled in against him. His left arm curled under his head. He couldn't figure out where to put his right arm. She reached over and took his hand and pulled it up around her near her neck, snuggled a bit and, with a contented sigh, went to sleep.

Tommy lay there spooning with a girl. His erection was a demanding embarrassment, but she didn't seem to notice, which he had a hard time believing. After a short time, the warmth and the closeness quieted him. He realized this was the first time he had slept with a girl. He had had sex before, frantic awkward slamming in the back of his mom's car, but he had never slept with a girl. He smiled as he drifted off.

They woke, still spooning. The sun wasn't up, but the sky was light. The light came through the red tent walls, washing everything with a pink hue. She'd twisted, pushed some errant hair out of her eyes and smiled.

"I have to pee," she said with a frown.

He smiled. It was obvious he needed to as well, his embarrassment back. He unzipped the sleeping bag and pulled his jeans on. She followed. The air was cool but not cold. He opened the tent flap, and she peered out.

No one else was awake. There was a mist drifting on the surface of the perfectly flat lake.

A SINGLE ROUND

"Race ya!" she said, and she bolted for the trees to the right. Laughing, he ran to the trees a bit further back of the camp, not wanting to get too close to where she was. When he returned, she was already back and was in the sleeping bag.

Tommy noticed his T-shirt and her jeans in a pile next to the sleeping bag. He peeled off his jeans and carefully slipped into the sleeping bag. She was on her side looking at him, her hands under her head. He lay on his back; his arms were crossed outside the sleeping bag.

They said nothing for a long time. He was unsure of what she expected, and the silence made him nervous. He was about to ask her how she slept when they heard Kirk's voice faintly from his tent. He was pleading. They couldn't hear all the words, but it sounded like he wanted something, and Alice wasn't interested. This went on for a while, then Alice's voice came loud and clear, "No!"

Rebecca and Tommy looked at each other, stifling their laughter. In a minute, they heard Kirk stomp by. Tommy and Rebecca were face to face smiling, then she went serious, looked at his face and kissed him. He kissed her back. With slow movements mixed with giggles and kisses, they moved together. This wasn't sex. This was something entirely different. He got lost in her, her smell, her taste. Everything mixed in pink, long hair, soft fingers, even softer lips and after a time, a soft, slow deep sign, her head back. Seconds later, Tommy clamped down, stiff, and he groaned.

He fell asleep tangled in her. When he woke, she was gone.

He pulled his denim shorts and t-shirt on. The shorts were still a bit wet from the day before. He went out.

The sun was up in force. Everyone was awake. Most were in the water.

Kirk was out on a black tractor tire inner tube he had brought along. Alice was sitting on the beach talking with George and Leslie. Jason and Cooper were far out in the lake, probably right at the point the lake dropped off, and with them, laughing was Rebecca. She noticed him and waved. Tossing his towel and T-shirt on the sand, he started walking out. When he got close, she jumped at him, arms wrapping around his neck and kissed him. She pulled back and, with a laughing finger, pulled a stray hair from her lips. Her eyes took on a devilish look, then she splashed him and raced away. He caught her easily, and laughing, they started walking back to the beach.

Tommy spread out his towel and lay down. Rebecca had her towel and bag set down beside Cooper. She went to retrieve them. Tommy watched her walk. She had on a black string bikini top and a pair of jean cut-offs. He liked what he saw. She walked back to him, smiling and swinging her bag.

"So, what do you want to eat?" she asked.

"Donno, but I think I'm hungry."

"Ya, me too, but all we got is burgers and chips. I think I want something different for lunch. You know what would be great is pizza."

Jason and Cooper were just coming out of the water.

"Hey Jason, are there any places around here we could get pizza?" Tommy asked.

"Ya, there's a truck stop maybe half an hour away. My pop says they got pretty good pizza," Brian said

"Well, you up for a pizza run?"

"Sure, let me get dressed. Who wants pizza?" Jason was always game.

As it turned out, everyone wanted pizza. They all piled into the cars and Jason's truck, but it turned out Dean's Mustang was stuck when they began leaving. The guys all got out and set to pushing.

After a few tries, Dean said, "Fuck it. Let's go, and we'll dig the 'stang out later."

So Kirk took Leslie, who seemed to have warmed up to Kirk again, Tyler, Alice and George. The little Datsun was full.

Jason with Cooper beside him. Dean and Leslie squished in the cab. Leslie gave George a little wave as she got into the truck.

Tommy and Rebecca sat in the box, cuddled up with a blanket.

"You fucking take it easy," Tommy told Jason

"Ya, ya don't worry. It's not far," Jason said, and they headed off. Tommy had to admit, Jason was taking it easy. Slow and steady.

A SINGLE ROUND

Rebecca was tight up against him. They talked and watched the Datsun following them. Tommy leaned over and kissed Rebecca.

"I'm glad you came."

"Me too. I really like you."

Tommy felt that weird heart thing then the truck lurched as if Jason had slammed on the brakes. Tommy was thinking about yelling at Jason when there was a scream from inside the cab followed by a horrible smashing sound. The truck lurched again. This time Rebecca and Tommy were flung from the truck box's back as the truck spun, then rolled into the ditch.

Tommy pushed himself from the grass at the side of the road. He didn't know where he was. He had lost his shoe. That made him mad. He liked those shoes. There was something wrong with his left arm. It hurt, and he couldn't move it. He wanted to go home. His mom would know what to do. He started walking. He wasn't sure how long he walked till the police car found him, driving up behind him, lights flashing. Two large men climbed out of the car and walked up to him. They asked a lot of questions that he couldn't understand. He just wanted to go home. They said they would take him home, so he went with them.

In the days that followed, he found out what had happened. When the truck had come around a curve in the road, a deer had jumped out, Jason had braked and turned, but the deer crashed through the windshield, killing Leslie and Dean instantly. The truck hit the ditch and launched Rebecca and him into the air. Rebecca died when she hit the pavement. Her neck was broken. The truck came to rest upside down in the ditch. Jason and Cooper died, stuck in the cab. They drowned in the water in the ditch.

George had managed to get the driver's door open but couldn't reach Leslie. He kicked at the windshield but couldn't break it. He watched her through the windshield as she drowned.

Tommy stayed in the hospital for a few days. He had hit his head, broke his left arm and was in shock, but when the doctors said it was OK. His parents took him home. He was numb. He walked through those next few weeks in a haze. The funerals were endless. He kept thinking about Rebecca's guitar at Stoney Lake getting wet. He woke in the middle of the night screaming, not sure what he was dreaming.

Then George committed suicide.

Tommy went to his funeral and thought he had had enough of funerals. He never wanted to ever go to a funeral again.

He stayed at home. He didn't play his guitar.

Kirk and Tyler came by. They talked, and Tommy listened, and they went away. Alice came a week after George died, but she just sat on his bed and sobbed for a while and left.

A couple of weeks later, Tyler came by again. He and Tommy had never really hung out. Tyler was Dean's friend. They sat in Tommy's room and just talked. The summer was slipping by. Tyler was talking about college. He thought maybe he'd become an electrician or maybe an engineer. He wasn't sure, and somewhere in the middle of Tyler's one-sided conversation, Tommy picked up his guitar and played a lick from the opening of 'Over the Hills and Far

Away." He stopped when he realized what he was doing. He started to cry and put the guitar down. After a while, Tyler left.

But Tyler kept coming back, and Tommy started to look forward to his visits. He started to pick up the guitar again, and things seemed to be getting better.

Tyler came one day with a new, new to him car he had bought at Carson's. It was a white Toyota with a stick shift. He wasn't very good at it, but he tried. They drove to the mall and walked around. Tommy hadn't been back to the mall since the day Jason and Mary Ann broke up. He felt off. Nothing felt familiar, and yet it was.

They went to a restaurant to have a burger.

"You ok?" Tyler asked.

"Ya, I just haven't been here since it happened."

"Ya, I get it. I miss them. Jason was an ass, but I miss him,"

"Ya, he was. I miss them. "

"You got close to Kirk's cousin. What was her name?"

"Rebecca." Tommy felt he might start crying. Tyler noticed

"I'm sorry. I didn't realize. It's her you miss."

Tommy couldn't speak.

"Why don't you talk to the Judge?" Tyler's joke fell flat. And he kept talking, but Tommy wasn't hearing him. An idea was drifting in his mind.

Rumours had spun around for years that if you went to a certain crossroads at midnight, a man would come to grant your wish. Most people laughed it off as a fun legend. A scary story that you can tell around a campfire. But Tommy started to think it might be real.

Cautiously he started asking questions. One story that came up more than once was about a man some ten years ago who went to the crossroads to make a deal. It hadn't gone well, but if he was still around, he might be able to tell him something about the Judge and his deals.

A chance meeting at a gas station gave Tommy a clue. He and Tyler had stopped for gas on the north end of town, and Tyler was surprised to see the mechanic was a brother of a girl he had dated.

They laughed and talked to the mechanic; his name was Dusty.

"Hey, ya wanna taste sum shine?" Dusty grinned. "It's the best ah ever tasted."

They both laughed and said sure. Dusty seemed very excited and returned with a glass jug half full of a clear liquid. Dusty had three Dixie cups. He poured a small amount into each.

Then with as much ceremony, he could muster, Dusty said, "Bottoms up," and threw the shine back. Tommy and Tyler followed suit. They both expected a harsh throat-burning gulp of fire but what they got was a warm, easy drink with flavour. It truly was an amazing shine.

"Fuckin' A. This is amazing" Tyler smiled and looked at Tommy. Tommy had never tried shine before, so he had no real way of knowing the difference. He did know it tasted amazing and wanted more. They both held their cups for seconds. Dusty laughed and poured a small amount in each.

"This ain't cheap, and it's hard to get. The dude who brews it only does small batches, and it's gone."

"Shit, man. This is fucking amazing. You got to hook me up," Tyler said.

"Ah, man. I dunno. I get it from Billy, one of Jacob's drivers. You know Billy, ya, you know him. Bill Gibbons."

Tyler thought about it then, "Yes, I remember him. Bit of a yahoo but an OK guy. Well, how can I get ahold of him?"

"Look, give me your number and next time he comes to town, I'll pass it along. If he calls, he calls,"

"Give us another sip," Tyler asked. Dusty grinned, and it looked like he wasn't going to. Then, with a chuckle, he pulled the cap off and gave them each another small sip.

"It sure is fine shit." Tommy said, "What's the guy's name that's brewing this up?"

"His name is Jacob. Story goes he sold his soul to the devil for the recipe."

Tommy perked up and said, "I would love to meet this guy"

A SINGLE ROUND

"I doubt if that would make you happy. Not a friendly kinda guy. Biker and scary as shit. I met him once, and that was enough for me. Huge motherfucker with a long black beard."

"See what you can do, would you do that?"

"Ya sure OK. I'll ask, but don't get yer hopes up."

"Thanks, Dusty," Tyler and Tommy tossed their cups in the trash.

"Thanks for the taste,"

A couple of weeks later, Tyler called Tommy to tell him Dusty had called.

"He said he talked to Billy. Dusty was changing Billy's alternator for him, and he'll be back on Tuesday to pick it up. If we were they we could talk to him,"

"Anything about the Jacob guy?"

"Naw, but Billy's got a straight line to the good stuff,"

They agreed they would have to be there to try to score some of that fine shine.

Billy turned out to be a kinda doughy kid who shuffled, rubbed his nose and kept removing his cap to push back his greasy hair. He was not much older than Tommy. He smiled and said, "Dusty says you guys are cool, so, sure, when the next batch comes out, I could get you some. Probably next week, but it's up to Jacob. He works to his schedule. "

"Any chance of meeting Jacob?"

Billy laughed, "No chance. He's a very private kinda dude," then with a grin, "but if you show up at the Ol' Scratch Taven out on 11 on a Thursday night, that's wing night-you might just catch him," There was mischief in his eyes.

The next Thursday, Tyler and Tommy headed for the Ol' Scratch. They drove for an hour and a bit. They were nervous but excited. They pulled off highway 11 into a gravel parking lot. The lot was full. They rolled around and managed to squeeze the Toyota in beside a huge truck that towered above Tyler's little white car.

They walked, runners crunching on the gravel to the neon laced bar. They both chuckled at the devil holding the bikini chick that buzzed in neon above the Ol' Scratch Tavern.

From outside, the noise coming from the bar was daunting. They stepped up and opened the door just as a huge guy in leathers stumbled out. He nearly knocked them both down and never noticed them. They looked at each other, second thoughts written on their faces, but Tommy was determined.

He stepped up, pulled the door open and walked in. Tyler grabbed the door before it closed and followed. Inside, they were met by a wall of sound. The bar was full, beards, bellies, and ball caps for as far as they could see. They pushed through to the bar, and their mouths dropped open. The bartender was by far the best-looking woman either of them had ever seen. She came up to them. They watched her walk over, stunned. She smiled, completely aware of her effect, "What kin I getcha?"

"Couple of beers," Tommy said

"You old enough there, hun?"

With a sign, Tommy and Tyler pulled out their driver's license and showed her. She nodded and went off and was back in a second with two beers.

"You running a tab or cashin out?"

Tyler pulled out a twenty. She took it and dropped the change on the bar top.

"Hey, you know a dude named Jacob?"

She smiled. "Ah hun, you don't want to wake that dog. He bites,"

"I need to ask him a question,"

"Hun, serious. Just leave him be,"

Tommy leaned forward, the desperation and pain on his face "I NEED to ask him a question"

A SINGLE ROUND

She smiled sadly. "OK, hun, OK," she looked around the bar, then she pointed. "See the mountain over there? That's Brian. He's tight with Jacob. Jacob will be over there. He's the one with the huge beard in leathers. He's the only motherfucker that'd wear his Colours in here!"

Tommy looked where he pointed. The man was truly a mountain of a man. He towered over the other's, a big grin on his face. The beer he held looked small in his hand. His laugh echoed across the bar.

"Jeeez, what the fuck is that?" Tyler asked when Tommy pointed him out.

"That's Brian. If she's telling the truth, Jacob will be with him." Then a shift in the crowd and Tommy saw him. Jacob was sitting, his chair pushed back, his face shadowed by the green ball cap pulled low on his head. He had 'fuck off' written all over him. As Tommy watched, Jacob stood and put his beer down and headed across the room. Jacob was tall and rangy. He had on an old black leather jacket and jeans, heavy boots and a denim vest over the jacket. There was a large patch on the back of the vest that Tommy had never seen before. It was a skull, but it was something else as well. It looked like it said "The Jurors."

Jacob walked with an easy swing, unhurried. He moved through the crowd, people melting out of his way.

Tommy moved without really deciding to. He pushed and ducked through the crowd and came up beside Jacob just as he was about to turn down the hall to the can.

"Jacob, I need to ask you a question,"

Jacob paused and looked at Tommy, "Fuck off," he said and turned to walk away.

"I need to ask you about the Judge."

Jacob stopped. He shook his head and turned. Then he walked toward Tommy with violent intent in his stride. He grabbed Tommy by his jacket, lifted him off his feet and walked him backward through the crowd. Men and tables were pushed out of the way. Jacob used Tommy's body like a ram. Men cursed, ready to fight, then seeing it was Jacob moved back. Frank, the Ol' Scratch owner, wondered how much damage Jacob was going to do this time.

Jacob stopped when Tommy slammed against the bar. Jacob pressed into Tommy's face, still holding him off the ground.

"Jacob, he's just a kid." the bartender touched Jacob's arm.

Tommy could have sworn he heard Jacob growl. Then Jacob dropped him.

The entire bar was watching, sure they were going to see the little shit get a whoopin. No one fucked with Jacob unless he was looking to be put down, but instead, Jacob asked, "What the fuck do you want with the Judge?"

At the sound of the Judge's name, suddenly no one wanted to hear the rest. They all turned away and busied themselves with not listening.

"I want to make a deal." Tommy stood tall and tried to look like he knew what he was saying. Jacob looked down and smiled. It was a smile with no warmth or humour.

"Then you are a fucking idiot." and he turned and walked away. Tommy stood there. He didn't have the fight to follow or push any further. Tyler was beside him.

"Come on. Let's get out of here." Tyler pulled at Tommy's arm. Tommy let himself be led from the bar. A few people watched them leave, but none bothered them. Tommy's head was down as Tyler hurried him out the door and into the parking lot.

"Hey, just a sec." It was the beautiful bartender.

Tommy turned and looked at her. She walked down to him.

"Why you asking about the Judge?"

"I need his help."

"Well, the Judge ain't there for helping folk, but if you have a powerful need. Take 11 west for a quarter mile, then turn south at the turn off beside the gas station. Six miles exactly, you'll come to a crossroads. Be there before midnight and wait. He'll show." She turned and walked away. Before she went back into the bar, she turned back, "Good luck, kid."

Tommy didn't speak the whole way back to town. Tyler didn't

seem to notice. He chatted excitedly about the near-miss they had just escaped. It was going to be a great story to tell.

A few weeks later, Tyler met Tommy in a bar near Tyler's place. They hadn't seen each other since their 'adventure,' as Tyler called it. Tyler ordered a beer and burger. Tommy had a beer in front of him, but he wasn't drinking.

"I went," Tommy said.

"Went? Where?" Tyler was watching the waitress pick up a napkin she had dropped and was definitely not listening.

"To the crossroads."

"What... Wait! What?" Now he was listening, "What the fucking hell did you do that for. Are you fucking kidding me?"

"Nope."

Tyler sat back, shaking his head, "Well fuck... and?"

"It's real. It's all real. He came. We talked, and I made a deal."

"Wait, you made a deal. What the fuck do you mean you made a deal?"

"Tyler, you swear too much." Tommy smiled, still looking down at the tabletop. "I sold my soul to the devil. That's who The Judge is. He is the devil. I sold my soul to the devil."

Tyler sat, not knowing what to say.

"Ok, you went to this crossroads place at midnight and what? The devil appeared with horns and a pitchfork all in red?"

"No, he drove up in a 68 GTO. He was a tall man in a fine suit."

"Ok, what did he say? What did you 'sell your soul' for?"

"Well, at first, he didn't want to do it, but then he said he could do it, but it would take a bit of time. He offered me a standard contract. Whatever I wanted for 6 months, 6 days and 6 hours, then I was his. Body and soul."

"Wait a fucking minute. You're serious!" Tyler leaned forward. "What did you ask for?"

"I asked him to bring Rebecca back."

"You did what?!"

"He said it would be done in a week." Tommy smiled and looked at Tyler.

"Ah, Shit, man, I thought you were serious. Yer just fucking with me.

"No, I did it. She's coming back to me.

Tyler laughed again

"Sure, sure. I hope you made sure she comes back as she was not as she is right now unless you're into maggots." He laughed, and Tommy frowned.

Tommy woke, nearly sitting bolt upright in bed. In the dark, the alarm clock's glowing red numbers told him it was 3:36. Something had woken him. He had been having this dream. His heart was pounding. In the dream, he was being chased by what. He couldn't get it. A person. A thing. Jason had told him to run. To get the hell out of there. But his feet seemed to be wrapped in heavy wet pants. He could hardly move, and something was getting closer.

He had to piss. He flung the covers off him and rolled onto the floor. It was cold. He danced to the bathroom in the dark. The dream slipping away. His heart slowed.

When he flipped on the light, he thought he heard a sound outside. He froze. He listened. He was looking at the floor listening, then looked up and caught his reflection in the medicine cabinet and jumped. He laughed at his foolishness.

Tommy walked over to the toilet, lifted the lid and let fly.

A sound.

Tommy stopped pissing. He had heard a noise. He was sure. Cock in hand, he listened.

A sound. A scuff outside the house. He started. Something

was outside, right outside the house, under the bathroom window. He stepped back, listening hard.

Another scuff like someone or something was dragging its feet as it walked around the house. Looking for a way in.

Tommy took another step back then ran to his room. Frantically he pulled on his jeans.

His parents were away for the weekend. Normally, that would be something to celebrate, but here and now, it wasn't. He was alone in the house.

He sure as shit, wasn't he going to turn on any lights. Carefully he crept down the hallway. Fingers lightly touching the walls so he wouldn't bump into anything and let whoever or whatever was outside know that he was here.

Slowly he made his way to the living room. He was standing there, toes in the shag carpet straining to hear. A shadow passed the living room window slowly. The streetlight made a crisp shape on the living room window curtains. It was a small shape., a shape he recognized.

Tyler's words rang in his ears, and all his fears came flooding into his mind. She was back! It was her. It was Rebecca. His Rebecca. The Judge had done it.

There was a light knock on the front door. Tommy ran to the door. He stopped. He listened.

"Tommy?" The voice was rough like a heavy smoker. "Tommy?" He looked at the lock on the door. It was locked. There was another knock on the door, stronger this time.

"Tommy?" She coughed. It sounded deep and wet. "Tommy, let me in. I'm cold."

Tommy reached for the door.

There was a bang against the door. He stopped his hand inches from the door.

"Tommy, my love. Let me in."

He took a small step backwards and lowered his hand.

"Tommy, why won't you let me in?"

There was a noise at the door he couldn't recognize. Then he did and realized it was scratching. It was fingernails clawing at the door.

"Tommy, let me in."

Tommy took another step backwards, hands at his side.

They were linked, the Judge had said, forever. For as long as they lived there were connected, locked together as one person. Tommy had given some of his life for her to come back.

Tyler's words kept running in his head.

"But you didn't ask for her to come back as she was! You just asked for her to return to you. The Judge is a very literal guy. It's his little pleasure. He gives you what you want, exactly what you ask for. She'll come back to you, sure, but she's been dead now for months. In the ground with worms. If she comes back like that...!"

Tommy stared at the door, rooted to the spot. There was a bang on the door. He jumped.

He turned and ran. His shin smashed into the edge of the coffee table. With a yelp, he crashed to the floor.

"Tommy. Let me in."

He scrambled to his feet and raced down the hall to his parent's room.

He was blinded when he flipped on the light. He ran to the clothes closet and opened the door. It had a clean laundry smell. He dropped to his knees and started shoving the boxes filled with family photos aside. He knew it was here. He had seen it. It was somewhere here.

"Tommy, we can be together, just like the lake."

He found it! He sat back on his heels and pulled it out. He was surprised at its weight as he always was. He rested the shotgun on his lap. It was black and cold. He looked at it. It was the only thing he could think of. It was a way, a way out.

"Tommy, What's wrong? Don't you want to be together?"

It was a way, but the gun was empty. He set the gun beside him on the carpet and started digging again. There must be shells in here as well. After a minute, he had to admit there were none here. He

A SINGLE ROUND

remembered his dad had said you never store shells with your gun. You always store them separately.

Tommy looked around the room. The night table, the one on his dad's side. He got up and went to it and pulled open the drawer. There was all kinds of stuff, papers, letters, a girlie magazine. But no shells for the shotgun.

"Tommy. I'm cold. Please let me in."

Where would his dad hide them? He stood. He walked to the closet and picked up the gun.

There was a bang on the door.

Tommy jumped at the sound.

The sock drawer! That's where!

He stepped to the chest of drawers and opened the top one. It was stuffed with white, pink, and lace. Nope. He opened the next one. It was filled with black and dark brown. Yes! He dug around one-handed, and there it was, a cardboard box. He pulled it out. It was bright yellow and had a big red 'W' on the side with 'Winchester' in red above that. There was only one shell left. It'll be enough. It would only take one round.

He dropped to his knees and broke the gun open. He slipped the shell in. It slid in perfectly. It was meant to be there.
He paused, then he stood. He didn't hurry. He walked carrying the heavy black dangerous thing. He knew what he had to do. Knew deep down. Once it was done, he'd be free.

He walked across the living room carpet and stopped.

"Tommy, please. Please let me in. The Judge promised"

Tommy imagined her then, not as he remembered her - a bright tanned beautiful girl with big, searching eyes - but as a dark muddy, half-rotten thing with dead eyes and lips pulled back in a parody of a smile. He set his jaw and reached forward. He was going to fling the door open and pull the trigger. It was that simple. Done!

"Tommy, he promised we'd be together forever." Her voice was quiet now, pleading.

He stopped his hand inches from the lock. The gun barrel dipped.

"Forever." Tommy paused. The gun barrel dipped further. A voice in his head asked, "if she's dead, how can you kill her?" And he knew the answer. He couldn't.

He stepped back. He knew what he had to do, and he began to cry. He cried for himself. He cried for his mom and dad. He cried for Rebecca.

There was a loud bang on the door.

"Let me in!"

He turned and walked to the couch and sat. It was the only way. No other way at all. He thought of his friends. His plans. He was getting good at the guitar. He had so much he wanted to do.

He put the butt of the shotgun down on his mom's shag carpet and leaned the barrel of the gun to his chest, and found he couldn't reach the trigger. His arms just weren't long enough. He cried, sitting there frustrated and scared.

Bang! She hammered on the door, screaming, "LET ME IN!" Tommy set the gun down beside him on the couch and slowly rose and went into the kitchen. He came back out with a broom. He sat, picked up the gun and slid the handle of the broom through the trigger guard.

"Tommy. I love you. Let me in." Her voice was quiet.

Tommy put the butt of the gun down on the carpet then pulled the barrel to his forehead, holding it with both hands. The broom handle rested against the trigger crossways to the gun. He rested his foot against it like a gas pedal.

"I love you too," he said for the first time in his life, and he meant it. He pushed hard with his foot as if revving his truck.

A SINGLE ROUND

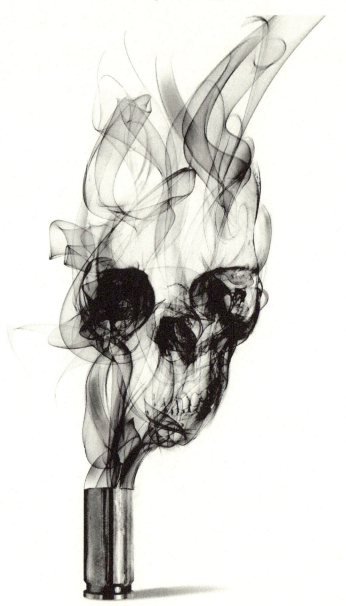

"What did you do?"

CHAPTER 3

BEING FAMOUS

The spit landed on her cheeks again as he yelled at her. Again. She stood perfectly still. She watched and waited. Her hatred, an actual thing inside her. How many times had she stood there waiting, listening?

His face reddened. His cheeks turned crimson, little pale white dots appeared. His eyes nearly bugged out of their sockets.

And the spit. Every word threw little drops of spit on her cheeks, her nose, her forehead. She stood and waited.

His screaming went on. He paced, arms gesticulated around, but always returned to jab at her with his finger and spit words at her.

She waited.

She reminded herself again that she had paid to be here. Had paid big to be right here on this spot. She paid more than anyone would know, more than anyone could ever guess. This is what she had wanted. This had been her heart's desire. She almost smiled at the thought and at the thought of her love.

No, she shut that down hard. She couldn't let that show on her face. She needed the hate in her eyes. She wanted it to show clearly. There could be no doubt in her face that she hated this man, hated him enough to kill him. It had to be obvious. She stood still, watching him. He made another circle around the tiny space, arms out wide, then back in her face. She waited. Soon now, she thought.

His face, very close to hers, growled out his final words. His lips pulled back like an angry dog's, revealing his big, surprisingly white teeth.

Still close, he stared hard into her eyes, brought the cigar he had been holding up to his mouth and pulled on it. She felt the heat from the ember. He blew the foul smoke into her eyes. They teared up instantly. The smell was sweet as it swam around her face. She didn't cough, but it took effort not to.

He stood and looked down on her, his eyes never leaving hers.

She waited.

Slowly she reached into her purse, her fingers finding the cold hard thing. They curled around the grip. She dropped the purse as she brought the pistol up and around. Her left hand followed and cradled the Beretta 9mm butt. She braced her feet square to the target, knees slightly bent, arms straight forward. In her mind, she ran through the checklist she had been taught. She sighted down the barrel with her dominant eye, her right eye. Tightened her stomach, braced for the recoil and squeezed the trigger. She noticed there was no surprise on his face.

The gun leaped in her hand, snapping her wrist up and back. The noise was a massive thing. She could smell the propellant—a burnt candy smell.

He flew from her. His arms and legs appeared to be left behind for a second as his body tore backwards. His arms extended straight out like he wanted to give her a hug. His feet left the floor and flew up.

She saw the soles of his shoes.

A SINGLE ROUND

She stood holding the gun out. Slowly she let her arms drop. She hung her head and waited. Her ears rang. It was very quiet.

She waited.

"Cut," the director's voice said. The room came alive. The first to her was the gun master. He took the gun carefully from her as Make-up arrived, dabbing the spit from her face.

She was grateful.

The man rolled about, reminding her of a turtle on its back as the effects persons helped him up from the crash pad.

He growled and swore, always complaining the harness had squashed his balls. He complained every time about his balls. Balls he had offered her on many occasions, and she had refused them most times. She looked at the director. He was watching the playback, his right hand on the back of his neck, his left on his hip. Nope, he wasn't happy. She could tell just from his pose. They'd have to reshoot.

She walked to her mark and waited. He walked towards her. His head thrust forward, shoulders pushed back, fists balled. Every time she wanted to step back from him. Every time she felt panic rising as he came on. It showed in her face. It made it all seem more real, she thought.

She knew he wasn't much of an actor. He had ties to organized crime, or at least it was widely rumoured. He looked it. He looked like a gangster.

He seemed even more aggressive this time. She always thought that. Maybe the director wanted her to be more scared.

He started his rant. He was in her face. She watched the redness cover his cheeks, and the spittle hit her. She hated the spit—flecks of foam at the corners of his mouth. The spit landed on her cheeks, her forehead, her nose, even her lips. Even her lips!

He ranted. He paced. His arms flew wide. He was coming close to the end of his speech.

She hated him. She hated the spit. Hated herself for the fear she felt. Hated herself for being afraid. He made her feel small. She knew the director wanted her afraid. He wanted her to look afraid. He wanted the camera to see she was afraid. And she supposed it did.

She waited. She waited as he jabbed his finger. She waited as he spat on her. She waited as he screamed his hateful words.

She waited for her time. On her mark, she waited. The finger jabbed. He ranted. He paced. He ranted some more.

She waited.

He pulled on his cigar. She squinted in the smoke.

Now she reached into her purse. Brought the gun up and around. Braced her knees, elbows locked, aimed and squeezed the trigger.

Her wrist cocked back, and her arm flew up with the recoil. The noise exploded out, loud and violent.

The man flew from her, feet flying up. She bent her head, arms lowering. She waited.

"Cut!"

The man swore. Always swearing, always complaining. Always complaining about his squashed balls.

She watched him struggle to get up. He rolled over to one side. The effects persons helped as best they could. He was heavy. He swore and finally got upright.

She hated him. She felt the hate. She felt the knot, the black knot in her chest.

"That's it! That's the look I'm searching for. That, right there!" said the director from the side in the partial dark.

She looked at him, at first not understanding, then she did. She looked at the director, looked back at the man. Her hate was wanted, even required.

She stood. The red face close, too close, and of course the spit. Always the spit. How she hated the spit. She waited.

He ranted. He paced. He ranted. He puffed on the cigar. The smoke rolled around her face.

She reached down. The purse. The coldness. The weight. The weight still surprised her.

She brought the gun around. Knees bent, braced and tight, her hate resting on her face, in her eyes. She aimed and pulled the trigger.

A SINGLE ROUND

The sound was huge. It filled the world. It felt louder than ever. It always did. The man flew backwards, legs swinging up. There was shock on his face. His eyes bulged, the whites circling his irises.

In slow motion, she watched him. Her hatred shrivelling as she saw the man's chest bloom with a dark red flower. It exploded, gore hitting her face, covering the spit. It soaked her face, her hair. It reddened her blouse. She watched him fly from her trailing gore.

She stood waiting. The man didn't struggle—no complaints about his balls. No movement. She stared at the man crumpled against the crash pad. She looked around to the director.

She saw him, mouth wide in a big 'oh.' She looked at the rest of the crew.

They all stared at her, shock on their faces. As if a switch was flipped, they started running, screaming. The gun master was beside her. He took the gun and slipped out the magazine. He looked at it, then to the director.

" They are blanks." He held the magazine out as if to show him. He looked at her, accusation in his eyes.

She looked at him, not understanding his reaction.

"What did you do?"

"I...I..," was all she could say.

The special effects crew milled about the horror that had been a man.

She stood still as people ran about talking. Inside, she couldn't believe what had happened was happening.

Her arms hung at her sides, her face fell slack, her eyes half-lidded, saw nothing. She was going into shock. She felt like she was dreaming. She felt removed. She felt as though she were looking down on the scene. She felt her vision shrink, blackness creeping in from the edges.

From a great distance, she heard herself say, "I think I'm going..." and she fainted. Dropping to the ground in an ungraceful heap.

When she woke, she was in an ambulance. A young man was leaning over her.

"How are you feeling?" he asked. His voice was calm and smooth.

"Fine," she said before she really had a chance to consider the question. When she did, she realized she was fine, but she remembered what had happened.

"Is he...?" She wanted to know, and yet maybe didn't want to know. She looked at him carefully.

"Is he dead?" she asked.

"Yes. I'm afraid so," he said, looking up and out the open door. He gestured to someone. She looked as a cop climbed into the ambulance.

She gave her statement after answering a bewildering number of questions.

As she answered the questions, she listened to her responses. It sounded bad. Even she could hear the false note. She was being completely honest, and yet it sounded like a lie. She hadn't been quiet about her feelings towards him. She said some things to her make-up people and maybe her wardrobe people. Maybe she had joked with the gun master. She had enjoyed shooting, enjoyed handling the gun more than was strictly necessary.

And people had known about her occasional indiscretion with him. And maybe she knew he had taken up with another actor in the cast, and yes, that actor was younger than her. That wouldn't look great.

All in all, it didn't look good. She wasn't worried. She was safe. She had a deal. She had made it a few years ago. She had gone to the crossroads near her hometown like so many around there had.

She had been talking to her best friend late at night on the phone about her dream to be an actor. This wasn't the first time. It was something she told anyone who would listen. Her dream had even been written in the yearbook every year since Grade 9. Her friend had heard the same thing a hundred times and finally suggested she go to the crossroads and get it over with. That stopped her in mid-sentence. She looked at her phone.

A SINGLE ROUND

"What?" she asked. She couldn't believe what she'd just heard.

"Just head over to the crossroads and get The Judge to make you an actress," her friend had said.

Later she lay on her bed thinking. She could. She could just jump on her bike and ride over there and just do it. A quick glance at her watch told her it was just after 11.

"It was a stupid idea," she told herself even as she started putting her runners on.

Her parents were in their bedroom. They weren't sleeping, but she wasn't afraid they'd hear her. As usual, they were fighting.

She went downstairs and out the door.

The crossroads were close. A few minutes down the road is what she had heard—the Judge's crossroads, where you go to make a deal. Where you got what you want, everything you want. Your heart's desire.

Her heart's desire. She remembered that night. She had waited, not expecting anything hoping she was wrong, terrified she would be right. She stood holding her bike, staring into the night.

When the black car slid up beside her, she breathed out. She hadn't realized she had been holding her breath.

The man who rose from the car and walked up to her had the most amazing smile. It shone in the gloom. She could still see that smile as if she had seen it just a minute ago. That smile had been the measure of every man she had ever dated. They all fell short next to its memory.

She watched his mouth as he spoke, watched the smile. It electrified her. She looked up and fell into his eyes. Liquid and dark with unimaginable depth. She smiled. The monster she was told would be here waiting to take from her everything was beautiful.

She was smitten. A schoolgirl crush of such power, it could, would consume her. She realized he had asked her a question. She hadn't heard.

"Umm... what?" She felt stupid.

His smile warmed, and his eyes twinkled. "What is your heart's desire, my dear?"

"You," she said, the first thing that came into her head, "I want to be a famous actress."

He stepped closer. She could feel his warmth.

"Done," he said, his voice like warm honey.

Her body vibrated at the memory. In the dark, on a lonely road at the crossroads, she gave herself to him. Gave more than just her soul. She dedicated herself to him. She was in love; with all the overwhelming power a 15-year-old girl could muster. This love, this power, was a pure bead of heat in her that would stay for the rest of her life.

Now some ten years later, she held this fervour, as precious as it had always been, a bead of fire that she fanned with her every breath. And in her heart of hearts, she knew he felt as she did. That he, a being of legend and myth; A being that every soul in the world knew of, whether they believed in him or not. He loved her with the same intensity as she.

So she wasn't worried about this confusion. Her deal would protect her. Her love hadn't softened nor weakened. If anything, her love for the Judge had grown with her, and now because of it, she knew she was safe. She would be a famous actress.

When the cop let her down from the ambulance, turned her and started putting on handcuffs while another cop read her her rights, a small shadow of doubt crossed her mind. She dismissed it immediately.

Sitting in the back of the police car as it pulled away from the studio, she looked out on a chaotic scene. There were photographers everywhere, snapping furiously as she passed. News vans pulled up at the side of the road.

And it hit her. She was about to get her wish, her dream. She was going to be a famous actress. She would be everywhere, her name on everyone's lips.

It was the twist that The Judge was famous for. He never handed you what you wanted. He always turned into something of a nightmare version of your deepest desire. She hung her head and began to cry, not for her twisted dream but for the loss of what she had had. Her love was not returned. The loss and betrayal were sour in her mouth. That smile, that beautiful smile, was the devil's smile, and she had been deceived.

It was almost funny.

R A JACOBSON

...red-winged black bird called.

A SINGLE ROUND

CHAPTER 4

REDWING

Her pale fingers dragged in the water. They left little trails, little bubbles bobbed. Little eddies swirled around her fingertips. The spring sun glinted off the water. Her fingers pushed up small swells as though the water was thick. The water was cold, very cold. Ice still clung to the bases of some willow trees and reeds. It was very close to freezing.

The water was cold and very clear for the first few inches, then turned the colour of strong tea. It stained everything below with a rusty edge, darkening quickly, so the bottom was lost in a brown-black depth.

Her sisters paddled so she could lay her head on her outstretched arm and watch the water go by.

A red-winged blackbird called. The reeds scraped against each other, making a dry sandpaper sound. A light wind stirred the dry yellow-brown grasses.

Below the surface was a lattice of light brown dead reeds from last summer woven in an intricate pattern. Here and there, the uniform yellow brown was interrupted by a hint of green. Through the tea, the green had a rich intensity, as though it held the power to bring on spring. It was the herald of spring.

She watched as a string of bubbles drifted up from the bottom. In a week or so, this water would be crawling with the squirming many-legged things that would become many-legged other things that flew. That buzzed and sometimes bit. Most were grey brown, sometimes spotted with black or white. Occasionally a tiny fleck of bright red would race across a leaf or the mud at the bottom. She loved this flash of brilliant red in a muddy world, a mite or something like that. It always felt like a surprise or a gift. She anticipated the sight of them every February when winter seemed to have settled in and would never leave; when spring seemed to be so far off, it might never come.

She would imagine that quick flash of red.

Her sister, Betty's paddle, left small vortices that slid past her fingers, stirring up bits of leaf and plant detritus. Her strokes were quiet, slow and rhythmic; she, like all of them, was an experienced canoeist.

Ever since they were small, they had gone out on the water as a family. There had always been six of them. They would drag the canoes from the garage as soon as the ice left the water. It was a family tradition.

She looked up when her sister stopped paddling. Her paddle made a deep thump that she felt more than heard. Now, both sisters had stopped paddling. She sat up and looked where they were looking off in the dry cattails. A red wing perched on a tall, dry reed that bent under its weight, bobbing slightly.

A SINGLE ROUND

Its quick eyes flitted as it watched them. Its black body shimmered with highlights of dark blue, but it was its shoulder that excited her. It was a bright, unreal red. It was too special to be here. It didn't belong in this marsh, this slough of mud grey light.

She looked up at her sister's back. Betty's back. Red hair, pale skin. Almost doll-like, she was slight. She looked like all her sisters, like herself. She had a quick smile that rarely touched her eyes. It was as if the knowledge they carried kept happiness at arm's length.

This day was not a happy day. This was their father's last canoe ride. He rode in the other canoe with mom and her other sister, Cheryl.

She had been surprised when her mom brought him out in his little pale green cardboard box. She was surprised at how small the box was. How tiny a whole man could end up to be. She thought of how loud and big he had been. How he'd fill most every room, he stepped into. He would own the very air that surrounded him. He hadn't been a serious man, not a man of high ideas or even an important man. He was your friend. He was...had been everyone's friend.

She looked across the water at the other canoe that held him now. Cheryl and her mom had stopped paddling. They drifted smoothly as they looked at the blackbird. The quiet water reflected them perfectly.

Veronica watched her mom. She was so still. She was so quiet. It was unnerving. She set her paddle in front and watched the redwing. A few weeks ago, she had stopped, stopped everything. She just sat staring at the wall or watched her daughters move about the house. She seemed lost, but Veronica supposed that could be expected. She couldn't imagine what she was thinking. What she was feeling. What it must be like to lose him, to lose her husband after so much time.

He hadn't been the nicest man. He always seemed angry, on the brink of an explosion. He rarely blew up, but the potential was there lurking in his eyes, in the set of his jaw or the tension around his lips. Even when he was joking at the breakfast table with her sisters, it was there in the corners of his eyes, the hardness she never understood.

Generally, he was kind to them, not really becoming a father when they were born. Not mean, just not there, not interested. The girls had talked about it many times. They each had a theory, but they didn't know, not really. They had even got up the courage to ask their mom. She smiled and shook her head slightly.

"It's not his fault," she said and nothing more.

Veronica watched her, then looked up at her sister at the bow of the canoe. She was watching their mom, as well. She looked back at Veronica. Being one of the quadruplets, they often shared thoughts.

Veronica knew what her sister, all of her sisters, were thinking. They had decided before they left the house. They had decided without talking. They knew because it was their idea. They knew how sad their mom was. She was heartbroken. They knew their mom's marriage wasn't great. It had been strained before the sisters had come along. It got worse afterwards.

It was late in the afternoon when the two officers knocked on the door. Ginger answered the door. As soon as she saw the officers, all the sisters came from all points of the house. They could feel the trouble. Together they called their mom. The cops stood in the door, hats in their hands with sober looks on their faces. But there was something else. The sisters saw it. It sat in the corners of their eyes and at the edges of their mouths. Veronica watched the cops. The man glanced back at the woman. She looked up. Did she fight back a grin? Her eyes had lit up for sure. Was she laughing inside? When the male cop turned back around, he was suppressing a smile.

Veronica was sure. The sisters looked at her, to the cops, confused at what was going on.

Their mother came walking slowly forward, and she looked to

her daughters with a question in her eyes. She was scared. Her eyes were already tearing up. She dropped her head, stepped forward and looked at the male cop.

"Mrs. Laverne Forester?" he asked.

"Yes." Her voice was small, shaky and scared.

"Mrs. Forester. We are here to inform you that earlier today; your husband Bruce Forester was killed as he attempted to steal a car."

"Did you shoot him?"

"No, ma'am. He succumbed to an accidental gunshot." The cop nearly started giggling as he spoke. "He was deceased when we arrived."

"I don't understand."

"It appears he was attempting to smash the glass from the driver's side window with the butt of a shotgun when it went off." The cop was enjoying telling this story. It was a story he was going to tell a lot.

"I don't...," their mother started. The colour drained from her face, and she swayed. The sisters rushed in to catch her as her knees gave. The cop's smile vanished. He stepped forward to help catch her but stopped.

"It's OK, we have her," Veronica said, looking at the cop.

After several minutes, the cops finally left.

The next week was hard. Their mother was either crying or walking around numb. She hid in her room most of the time. The sisters brought her food and tea that she mostly refused.

After the funeral, the house remained quiet. The sisters did what they could. They sat in the front room and waited. They cooked, cleaned and looked after things. They waited.

They put their father's ashes on the table beside the TV and waited.

When the weather warmed enough in early April, they agreed it was time.

They pulled the canoes down from the rafters in the garage.

They prepared. They talked to their mom. She agreed. It was a good idea.

"He would like that. He always loved a spring canoe trip," she smiled at her daughters when they suggested it. They were good girls.

The redwing called again. The sisters looked at each other. Was it time? Veronica looked at Ginger, to Cheryl, to Betty. They looked back. It was time.

"My girls," their mother said, "he was a good man. I know you never got to see that in him. But he was a good man. He wanted a family so much. And we tried for so many years," she held the urn in her arms, "So very many years."

She looked up at her girls. They brought the two canoes beside one another, and the sisters held them together.

"I'm sorry. I couldn't think of anything else to do," their mom said, looking back at the urn. "I wanted a family too. I wanted children more than anything."

The sisters looked at each other.

"I know you hated the idea, but it was the only way. The only way." Their mother spoke to the urn, then out across the water. She looked at her daughters.

"I had to. He knew, of course. Four little red-headed girls show up. Perfect little girls. You all were so small. He just couldn't get over it. He couldn't get used to you. He hated where you came from."

The sisters gathered close. They leaned in and let her talk. She needed to talk; they knew.

"But I needed children. So, I did what I had heard others had done. I went to crossroads south Highway 11. And you were there waiting for me when I returned home. My perfect little gifts, and all I had to do was make a deal."

"It's time," the sisters said in unison.

Their mother leaned over the edge of the canoe and poured out the ashes. Some of it sank, some floated, and some were caught by a light gust of wind and was carried out into the slough.

Their mother stayed, watching the ash move away from them.

"Bye," she said and touched the water.

That's when the canoe tipped. Their mother and Cheryl plunged into the frigid water.

The remaining sisters watched. The surface became still. A few bubbles broke the surface, it stilled once again.

Minutes passed.

More minutes passed.

Cheryl's head surfaced. The sisters looked at each other. They were sisters. Always had been, always would be.

Cheryl climbed into the canoe. They stood and undressed.

The canoe rocked.

They looked at each other's pale, identical white forms with shocking red hair; they arched their heads back and stretched out their arms.

They blurred. Their bodies shifted, darkened, and shrunk. They vibrated violently, then four red-winged blackbirds sat on the edge of the canoe. They looked to each other, their quick eyes flitting about, with an easy jump they took to the air. The slough was quiet, dry rasping sounds, a slight breeze and far off the sound of a red-winged blackbird.

R A JACOBSON

It growled as he came in

CHAPTER 5

DOC's CHOICE

Jacob was angry, No scratch that. He was pissed. He was 17, soon to be 18, and he was more pissed off than any 17-year-old had ever been in the history of 17-year-olds. He was fuming, ready to take on the devil. That wasn't an expression; it was the literal truth.

The Judge had fucked him and fucked him good. He wanted revenge on the devil; he just didn't know how he would get it.

His truck was no help. It was on the Judge's side, which was obvious. It was a demon in the shape of a truck. He fucking hated the truck, Clyde.

For a couple of days, it had been so good. He had rolled into the school parking lot, and everyone looked. It was fucking cool. Here he was driving a brand new shiny black 1977 Chevy half-ton. Even the jocks had noticed. Even the nerds noticed. The football team seemed to pause as he drove in for the first time. The photo club all turned and looked, a couple even snapping a photo. It was fucking awesome.

He walked down the hall, feeling like a king. That was, of course, until people found out how he'd got it. Then they laughed. Who would be stupid enough to sell their soul to the Judge for a truck, even a truck as nice as Clyde? They laughed out loud until after a few fights. Jacob beating on boys twice his size. Jacob stood unharmed, and Clyde had a few dents.

That is when Jacob discovered that any hurt he received didn't show up on his body but on Clyde's. He was invincible. Jacob had always been quick to use his fists; now, he gained a reputation. They left him be. Those that didn't quickly realized how fast Jacob turned to violence. They still chuckled, but now it was behind his back.

Then it all changed. Jacob's tragedy became fully realized. Some friends stayed true to him, but most shunned him. He became a ghost in the school, a cautionary tale to tell in whispered corners.

After Mary Lou had been killed, he went back to the crossroads every night for weeks, most times with a bottle and his pa's gun. His pa's gun was a chrome long barreled 45. It was a big heavy thing that his pa called his bear gun. He looked for the man in the shiny car to make him pay for her death.

One night he had been drinking and playing with the gun. It had slipped from his fingers. He had bent forward to catch it, when it struck the transmission tunnel. The gun went off. The roar inside the cab deafened him.

For a minute, he couldn't think. He blinked. His ears rang. The smell of propellant had an acrid bite.

When he could think, he reached down and picked up the gun. He wasn't sure where the bullet had gone. He looked around the cab. There in the cab's roof was a neat hole that had already started to close up. He felt the pain in his ear. He touched his ear and was surprised to see blood when he brought his finger back.

"Jeez, that was close."

He laughed out loud.

The next night he was back, gun in one hand, bottle in the other. He screamed. He cursed. He dared, he pleaded. He stomped. He paced, he waved the gun about; he swore he drank, and after hours, like most times, he'd pass out in the center of the crossroads, tear-stained and nearer to the gun each time.

How could he be alive, and she was dead?

It was his fault!

A SINGLE ROUND

The guilt and horror of it tore at him. Not at his soul because that wasn't his anymore, but at him, at his being. What made him, him? He carried his gun now, always. It was his assurance. His life was his. If he could take it at any time, then it was his. He owned it. After a time, he stopped going to the crossroads. The Judge never showed.

The heat of youth fueled his anger. He stormed through life. Righteous anger, his shield, his justification, and most people gave him latitude. Everyone knew his story, the loss of young love, true love. Something they had all lost never to recover, but here was a boy who had lost it not because he grew out of it but because it was brutally taken from him. A story for the ages. A Shakespearian tragedy writ real.

But it wasn't that. That is the romantic tale, one written down in a book. This was a foolish young boy that did something so stupid it cost his young girlfriend's life. And for what?

A truck? Well, no, not really. He sold his soul for the love of a girl. To give her a special gift, a grand gesture to prove his love. And the young are fond of the grand gesture.

Jacob spiralled. He became a shadow of himself. He drank. He fought. He searched for the Judge. Jacob never even considered that he was no match for the Judge, never thought that revenge was out of his reach. It was what he had to do.

Jacob's isolation fueled his anger. He spent hours sitting in Clyde, staring at the Judge's trailer. Brewing, cursing and drinking. The summer blurred past in an angry haze.

It was nearing the end of September when it reached a peak of sorts. Jacob had sat in Clyde drinking beer, staring at the little trailer surrounded by derelict cars. Rusted hills stacked and piled with only a narrow two-wheel path leading to the tree and the small trailer beneath it. For the Judge, it looked very unimpressive.

Jacob got out and pissed in the general direction of the trailer. He zipped up and made a drunken decision. He jumped into Clyde, fired it up and floored it. Clyde's engine roared to life, and they hurtled down the low hill.

"This is a really bad idea," Clyde said in Jacob's head.

Jacob ignored him and pushed harder on the accelerator.

And Clyde was right. Jacob never made it to the Judge's trailer. Nowhere close. He made it through the gate and past several rusted cars, but at the first narrow turn, he clipped a bumper of a derelict car. It hurtled Clyde and him into the air, spinning.

Jacob found out that the invulnerability he enjoyed swung the other way. Every dent Clyde received showed up on Jacob. Clyde's front fender crumpled, just as fast straightened as a massive bruise ran across Jacob's ribs.

Jacob was thrown through the windshield and landed on the roof of a crumpled old car.

Clyde sat in the narrow lane with a few dents from Jacob's injuries, but Jacob lay bleeding and bruised.

He lay there for some time, barely conscious. He felt himself being lifted by strong, surprisingly small hands. He was laid on the ground. Jacob opened his eyes and squinted up at a tall, thin, very handsome man bent over smiling at him.

"Ah Jacob, that looks like it hurts," then to someone else, he said, "put him in his truck. He can recover there."

Jacob felt the small hands again. He was roughly shoved into the cab of Clyde.

"You'll live. Don't come back, Jacob. At least not seeking some childish revenge." The Judge slammed the door.

Jacob woke slouched in Clyde's seat. He sat up and looked about. They were still sitting on the track that led to the Judge's trailer.

A growl made Jacob start and turn. Beside him, sitting on Clyde's seat, was the largest German Shepherd he had ever seen. As he looked, it growled low, but didn't snap at him.

He reached over and touched the collar. "Doc," it said.

Jacob backed out of the track and headed home. He was covered in bruises and still hurt, but nothing was broken. He needed to sleep.

When Jacob woke, he was in his room. He rolled over and sat up. He had a hangover, and he was sore all over. Last night was

a blurry mess. He had been angry, but that wasn't anything new. He was over at the Judge's.
Something, but it wasn't clear. He stood and nearly tripped over the massive dog lying on the carpet by his bed.

He remembered.

He reached down to pet the dog.

"So, can you talk in my head like Clyde?" Doc growled low in his throat. Just a warning, but it was apparent it could go bad quickly. Jacob pulled his hand back.

"OK." He stepped over the massive dog and went to the bathroom.

He winced. He stood in front of the mirror. He was black and blue from mid-thigh up to his armpit. He had a fine shiner. His left eye was swollen, nearly closed. The white of his eye was bright red. Kinda freaky. He had a piss and headed back to the bedroom.

The dog hadn't moved. It growled as he came in. Jacob grabbed his T-shirt, slipped on his underwear. He realized his jeans were partially under the dog. Shit. He pulled at one leg. The dog growled, its top lip shaking, ready to pull back. Jacob paused. With a quick yank, he tore the jeans free and bolted from the room. The dog growled but did not raise its head.

On the landing, Jacob pulled on his jeans and went down to the kitchen.

His Ma was in the kitchen as usual. She'll be baking something for sure. Once again, Jacob marvelled that his pa didn't weigh 300 lbs with all the cookies, pies and fresh bread he ate. Jacob sat at the small table.

His Ma said, "Morning," as she buttered a couple of slices of toast for him. She turned and nearly dropped the plate with his toast.

"What'n'hell happened to you?" She put the toast down in front of him. "You bin fighting agin?"

Jacob looked up, "Ya...Nah, not really."

"Well, yer pa needs some help in the garage. He doin' the brakes on the grain truck."

Jacob finished his toast and groaned quietly when he stood.

"Looks like you got the shit end of whatever stick beat on you." his Ma said.

Jacob walked to the porch and shoved his feet into his work boots. He heard his Ma call.

"Do up yer laces," just as the door slammed.

Jacob walked across the yard, his laces dragging. He went up to where Clyde was parked. He had a few dents and scrapes, but not bad.

He heard his Ma scream and swear.

"Who's fucking dog is this?" And Doc came running out. His Ma stood on the porch, yelling. Doc walked over to Jacob.

"He's mine," Jacob said.

"Well... well, he stays outside," she said, and with a wave of her tea towel, she went back in.

Jacob looked at Doc, who looked back, walked over to the garage and laid down in the doorway.

Jacob's pa stepped out of the garage beside Doc and looked to Jacob.

"Yours?"

Jacob walked toward him and nodded. His pa wiped his hands on a rag, looked at Jacob, then at the dog. He turned and went back into the garage and never mentioned it again.

Jacob spent most of the day washing parts, finding tools and listening to his pa swear. It was supper time when his Ma yelled for them to come in and wash up. Jacob was inside the cab, waiting to be told when to push the brake pedal. His pa moved around the truck with a tiny wrench, opening-closing the bleed valves till the air stopped hissing out. Each time Jacob pressed; the pedal stiffened.

Finally, his pa said, "good."

Jacob jumped down and headed for the house. Doc was nowhere in sight. Jacob noticed absently that many of Clyde's dents were gone or much smaller. In the bathroom, Jacob pulled up his T-shirt and looked at his bruises. They, too were looking much better, black, blue and now yellow, but he had to admit they were smaller.

Jacob washed and ate supper in silence, like every night. Only the clink of fork and knife on the plates. When he was done, Jacob's pa rose without a word and headed back to the garage.

Jacob sat for a few more minutes. He was finished but didn't like leaving his Ma alone so quickly.

"You going out tonight?" She asked as she cleared the table.

"Ya. Actually, I don't know. There's a party over at Brian's. His folks are out of town. But I don't know. Brian's bein kinda weird lately."

"Oh?"

"Ya, I dunno. He can be such an ass."

"Well, he's a lot like his father,"

Jacob laughed.

"Yes, Brian's father was an ass as well. Maybe I'll go see the ass himself after all."

Jacob went up to his bedroom. Doc was lying on the floor by his bed.

"How'n hell did you get up here? If Ma catches you, there will be some shit!"

Doc growled and closed its eyes.
Jacob changed into cleaner jeans and a t-shirt and went downstairs.

"You gonna take Clyde?" Ma called. She was sitting at the table playing solitaire, waiting for her bread to be ready to be taken out of the oven.

"Y s'pose."

"Well, don't drink too much and have a wreck. Ya know it's not that far ta walk."

"Ya k." Jacob shoved his feet into his boots and heard his Ma yell, "Tie yer laces!" as the door closed.

The sun was still up, but not for long. It cast long shadows across the yard. Jacob walked to the garage and watched his father tinkering.
After a couple of minutes, Jacob said, "I'm heading over to Brian's," Jacob turned and headed out of the garage. He heard his pa's grunt.

"So, you're heading to Brian's. Are you feeling up to it?" Clyde asked. Jacob was still getting used to Clyde's voice in his head. It had been several months, and it always made him jump.

"Ya. Still sore but getting better. So.." and he paused, not sure what he wanted to say,

"So, we are connected."

"You knew that," Clyde responded, "but I guess you didn't realize the whole of it. I took your damage. The reverse is true. You take my damage. Mind you, we both can take a hell of a lot of damage."

"Ya, I guess I hadn't really thought about it."

"We're not invincible by any means, and your little stunt was pretty stupid, but by tomorrow we'll be fine."

Jacob climbed into Clyde and started the engine.

"I'm still fucking mad at the Judge for what he did."

"Ya, I get that. I'm a demon, so I owe my allegiance to him, but..."

"But what?"

"I'm not sure. I've never been on this plane before, and I'm still not sure how everything works. It's weird. I'm feeling something toward the Judge that is... unfamiliar."

Doc walked past.

"What the fuck is that?" Jacob yelled

"Oh ya, you haven't seen Doc's true form. He's a hellhound. Through my eyes, you can see him plain. He's supposed to be watching you for the Judge, but I don't think he's really into it."

Doc lumbered past a massive dog-like beast with huge shoulders covered in black spikes. He had long sabre teeth and a tail like a giant rats.

"That's one ugly creature,"

Doc looked up and bared his fangs. They were nearly a foot long. He walked on.

"Just a suggestion, but I wouldn't piss him off," Clyde said.

Jacob pulled the truck into drive and headed down the lane.

The lane was a long straight gravel road that ended at the township road 78. Turning right would take them to 11, and the crossroads and turning left would take him to Brian's farm. He turned left and drove on.

It was a short drive. Brian's family farm, Jacob's closest

A SINGLE ROUND

neighbours. As a result, Jacob and Brian had been friends for as long as either could remember.

They turned off the road onto Brian's farm lane. Unlike Jacob's, it curved around a thicket of trees.

It was early, but there were already several trucks in the yard. Jacob pulled Clyde off the lane a little way from the house. He wanted to be able to leave if he needed to. He didn't want to get stuck behind other trucks.

He hadn't gone to too many parties since Mary Lou's death. He hadn't wanted to be around people. They either stared at him like he was a freak who had gotten away with murder or avoided looking at him because he had lost his true love. In either case, he was a tragic character. He couldn't stand their pity or their judgement.

Of course, there were the few that knew what really happened. The ones that were marked as well. The ones who had stood at the crossroads and made their deal. But they didn't talk to him or anybody. They all had reason to regret their deal, and most kept it secret.

When Jacob drove in Clyde, he could see them. Clyde windshield was Clyde's eyes, so to speak, and so Jacob could see through demon eyes. The people who had made deals were literally marked. They had a black smudge on their forehead as if someone had touched them with a finger covered in ash. He had seen that before, around Easter time, and the churchgoers walked around with ash on their foreheads. He was pretty sure it was a different thing.

Jacob had heard that the forehead was where the third eye, the eye of the soul, was, but he didn't know about that.

Jacob was surprised by how many 'marked' there were. After he saw them, he found he avoided them. He looked away when he met them, not wanting to meet their eyes.

Jacob stepped down from Clyde and walked to the house. There were people he saw in the windows. Jacob stopped and watched them laughing.

"So ya goin in or what?" Brian said as he stepped from behind the house. Brian was a tall, thin, slightly gangly boy with a long swinging gait.

"Hey, Bri. whatcha up to?"

"Getting some beer. There's a fire out back. You gonna stay?"

"Ya, I think so."

"Com' on, we'll get a beer and go by the fire." Brian headed inside, and Jacob followed.

So, Jacob decided to stay. He sat around the fire and didn't say much. Brian had pulled bales of hay up and placed them in a circle around a huge old tractor wheel that they had sunk halfway into the ground to make a fire pit.

Brian laughed and joked. He was having a great time. Jacob just couldn't get into it. The fire danced, casting twisting shadows on the laughing faces. It twisted the pretty girls into skeletal demons and turned the boy's faces beast-like. After a time, he got up. He couldn't take it. He waved to Brian, who seemed to be getting somewhere with a blonde girl Jacob didn't recognize. Brian didn't seem to notice.

Jacob stood and watched the party for a minute longer, then headed back to Clyde. He was just rounding the house when half the football team stepped around, heading for the fire. Gord was the star quarterback and had his own posse. He was cruel and loved the power he held. He also had a thing about Jacob.

"Shit," Jacob said quietly.

"Well, fuck! Look what we have here. The murderer that got away with it."

They blocked Jacob. Jacob was as tall as all of them, but he didn't have the bulk. They spent their spare time in the school weight room getting jacked. Jacob spent his working on the farm. Jacob had a spare ditch digger strength.

He just didn't want the hassle.

Jacob moved to go around them, and they moved, surrounding him.

Jacob stood still. He looked at Gord. "Really?" he said.

"Gord, you are such a fucking asshole."

Gord smiled a cruel dark smile, turned to look at his friends, then spun with a huge haymaker.

Jacob saw it coming a country mile away. He had time to

A SINGLE ROUND

decide what to do. He could easily duck it, or he could take it on the chin and let Clyde deal with the dent he would get.

Jacob smiled.

The fist turned Jacob's head but didn't stagger him. He looked at Gord and smiled.

"Hell, I thought you were strong being the big quarterback an' all."

Gord stood and looked confused. His hand hurt. He looked around at his friends, feeling exposed. He hit Jacob again. It had the same effect, which was none.

Jacob smiled. "That's it? Really?" He looked at Gord and smiled. This was fun.

In his head, he heard Clyde say, "Are you just going to let him beat on you?"

"C'mon, one more." Jacob stuck his chin out and closed his eyes.

When Gord hit him this time, he put everything he had into it. Jacob heard the bones break. Gord howled in pain, clutching his broken hand.

Jacob stood, his eyes still closed, his chin jutted forward. He opened his eyes,

"Oh, did you hit me?" Jacob smiled at the confused faces.

"Humm, that looks bad." He said to Gord, "Does it hurt?"

Gord was hunched over. His face was white. He looked up at Jacob.

He was furious.

"Well, this has been fun. You guys have a nice evening?"

Jacob walked around the gathered group and away from the party. The loud music, getting smaller as he walked through the dark, past the collection of pickups gathered in front of Brian's folks' house and found Clyde.

"Have fun?" Clyde asked.

"Ya." He said and smiled. He thought about it. It had been fun. Then it turned petty and small in his mind. Here he was using this curse he had asked for to humiliate a bully—a bully who, like so many people in the area, thought of him as a killer.

"Let's go home." Jacob climbed into Clyde. He drove slowly.

He wasn't drunk, just not interested in roaring along. Halfway home, there was a loud thump, and Clyde lurched. Jacob spun, looked in the box and saw Doc standing there looking at him. Jacob drove on, and Doc sat and watched the passing trees in the dark.

They pulled into the yard and parked. Doc jumped down.

"Night," Jacob said. After a pause, Clyde said, "Night." It was the first time Jacob had spoken to him like someone, not something. Doc followed Jacob.

"Oh no, you sleep out here," Jacob said to Doc. "Go sleep in the garage." Doc stood and watched Jacob go into the house.

A week later, Gord was found not far from Jacob's farm. He had been attacked by a bear, a usually ferocious bear. It may have been a grizzly, but they seldom came this far south.

They figured he had been out hunting. They found Gord's dad's hunting rifle cast into the field some hundred paces away. It was bent nearly in half the stock splintered by what looked like large claws. The cops were confused by the size of the claw marks and when he was killed. Hunters don't hunt at night, and Gord had died around midnight.

Whatever had killed him had to have been massive. Gord had been ripped to shreds. The pieces were scattered everywhere. The gossip around the school was that they found pieces of meat hanging from branches some 20 feet up. They never found his head.

The police chief and a couple of cops went straight to the school to talk with Jacob after they found Gord, or what they collected of Gord, near Jacob's farm. The police chief was Mary Lou's uncle, who was convinced Jacob was somehow responsible for her death. It didn't take much for him to look for ways to jam Jacob up.

They interviewed everyone who had anything to do with Gord. Gord's girlfriend had said Gord was real angry at Jacob and told them about the fight at Brian's party, but nothing had come of it. Jacob had been with his folks that night.

After school, Jacob climbed into Clyde.

"Do you know anything bout Gord?" Jacob asked.

"No, but I'll ask Doc," Clyde said.

"Doc?"

"Ya, I have a feeling he may know something."

"Do you talk?" Jacob asked. It had never crossed his mind that they would talk. They both were demons, so it made sense.

"No, not really. We're not the same kind of demons. He's more instinctual, but I can see some things if he lets me."

They drove back to the farm.

"I'll talk to him tonight," Clyde said as they drove into the farmyard.

The next morning Jacob was up early. He went downstairs. His Ma was already up and, in the kitchen, fresh bread and homemade jam. He sat, ate, smiled at his Ma and headed out.

Doc walked up to him when he stepped out. His teeth were bared. Jacob ignored him and walked past to stand close to Clyde.

"So?" he said quietly.

"You know if you practiced, you wouldn't have to talk out loud for me to hear you," Clyde said.

Jacob ignored the comment. "What did you find out?"

"Well, it's not really clear. Looks like from the images Doc showed me. He saw you getting hit at the party. He didn't like that. He thinks of you as his. I guess Gord was coming over here to shoot you."

"Shoot me?"

"Ya, that was what it looked like. Doc smelt him and went to check."

Jacob looked across the yard to where Doc lay. Doc's head came up. He looked at Jacob.

Jacob walked over to Doc. There was something under his paw. Jacob leaned forward. Doc bared his teeth. A low, threatening growl warned Jacob not to reach for the well-gnawed skull Jacob assumed once was Gord's.

Jacob stepped back. Doc watched him carefully and crunched down on the bone. It splintered.

Jacob turned. He could hear the crunching continue as he walked away. He walked into the garage.

His pa was rebuilding a tractor carburetor. He looked up then back to his work. Jacob didn't say anything, just watched for several minutes.

"I'm going over to Brian's. I'll be back to help later." His pa grunted but didn't look up. Jacob walked out of the garage and headed over to Clyde.

He climbed into Clyde and started it up.

"Heading to Brian's?" Clyde asked.

"Naw, just a drive. I got to think about this. I mean, Gord was an asshole, but this is wild." Jacob pulled Clyde into gear and started down the driveway. He glanced in the mirror and saw his father standing outside of the garage, wiping his hands on a rag, watching Jacob drive off.

In the mirror, Jacob saw something odd. It was like a cloud or a shadow of a cloud hovering over his pa. He stopped, looking at his pa. He thought he was seeing things.

"What's up?" Clyde asked.

"Donno," Jacob reversed and turned Clyde around to look through Clyde's windshield.

"Shit," Clyde said quietly.

"What is that?" Jacob asked.

Through Clyde's windshield, the cloud that hovered over Jacob's Pa looked larger, denser and looked like it was made up of wings. It suddenly disappeared. Jacob's Pa turned and walked back into the garage. Jacob drove Clyde forward.

"What was that Clyde?"

A SINGLE ROUND

"I'm sorry, Jacob. That is Death."

As Jacob watched, the shadow returned. It sank down to the ground, then grew into the shape of a man. Jacob stomped on the gas. Clyde leaped forward.

The shape solidified into a tall black man dressed in black. He looked at Jacob, smiled, and walked into the garage.

Jacob jumped from Clyde and ran into the garage. His Pa lay on his back on the ground in front of his workbench. The black man knelt on one knee beside him. As the man stood, great wings made of bone unfolded from his back. He looked at Jacob and melted into the air.

Jacob ran to his father. He was gone.

Jacob sat back on his knees and looked at the body that once was his father.

The next few days were wrapped in a fog. He walked through the world, barely aware of the people that came and went. He knew his Ma was sad. He heard her crying at night. She didn't yell at him anymore.

Things had shifted with Doc. Jacob was very wary of the dog, but his Ma seemed to like the company. Doc was even allowed in the house; in fact, she seemed to like having the dog around. Jacob didn't know what to do about it. If Jacob tried to move the dog, it growled, and Jacob sensed that it could actually hurt him. So he left it alone.

Clyde said that it didn't look like Doc was dangerous except for anyone that wanted to hurt his "pack."

"So, we're his pack?"

"Looks like it," Clyde said.

Somehow that made Jacob feel better. Doc started spending more time in the house with his Ma.

Jacob spent a lot of time sitting in Clyde pulled off 11, looking at the crossroads where he had lost everything. He had lost the girl he loved. He assumed it was payment for his deal. All deals with the Judge had their payment. Something about balance he had heard, and every time the payment was something horrible.

Jacob sat, thinking about his deal. Thinking about Mary Lou.

He wondered if she was his payment or was it his father. Was his father's death his payment? Was his father's death his fault?

As he sat, he thought. His hatred of the Judge grew.

He drove back to the farm. He found his Ma, sitting on the couch, staring out the front window at the fields that were her responsibility.

As she sat, Doc sat beside her. She petted him absently.

Jacob looked at her. She was all he had. He went to the kitchen and made supper. It wasn't much, just eggs, and toast. It was all he really knew how to make.

His Ma ate a bit. She was quiet. Doc stayed beside her. Jacob cleaned up and went out to the garage.

He stood in the middle of the garage. This was his Pa's. This was where he worked with his Pa, but it wasn't his, but it was. Now, this was his garage.

He looked around at all the projects that were not his, all the little things that his Pa was working on. All the things he was trying to fix. Stuff he was planning to get to, but now he would never get to them. Not ever.

He sat, overwhelmed, and he cried. He cried for the first time since his Pa passed. He cried like a small boy. He cried till he couldn't anymore.

It was late when he went back to the house.

"Night Clyde"

"Night Jacob"

Inside, Jacob walked through the kitchen. The house was dark. His Ma had gone to bed. He stood in the small, quiet house. It felt bigger without his Pa as if his presence had filled it up, and now it was empty. He felt the hollowness of the house, the hole his Pa had left in his world. A hole that would never be filled.

Jacob walked up the narrow stairs to his room. He looked around, but Doc was nowhere.

Jacob went to bed.

In the next few weeks, things became more normal. His Ma started cooking and finally started baking again.

Jacob took on projects his Pa had started. He worked from early in the morning till late in the evening. The garage would always

A SINGLE ROUND

be his Pa's, but now it was partly his. Now the work on the benches was his, and the farm became his. He worked like his Pa had, and he stopped thinking about the Judge and his hatred.

He had been fixing the starter on the old GMC truck, wondering how he was going to get the crops off before it rained or snowed. He had two hands driving combines. He had been driving one, but the GMC's starter had crapped out, so he was on his back trying to figure a way to get it to work when he heard a truck coming up the lane.

He looked from under the truck and saw a red half-ton pull up to the house.

His Ma, with Doc beside her, was standing on the porch. It was Mrs. Gibbons.

Jacob crawled from under the truck and started walking up to the house. He watched his Ma hug Mrs. Gibbons. A very unusual thing. His Ma wasn't a hugger.

He looked out in the field. His two combines were kicking up dust as they worked, but now there were two grain-trucks pacing along. They were emptying the hoppers. Mr. Gibbons and his boy, Billy, had come to help.

He smiled. He felt a wash of gratitude and relief come over him. His shoulders relaxed and came down. He hadn't realized he was clenched as tight as he had been.

They were going to get the crops in after all. Things were going to be ok.

Two years later, his Ma passed. When she got sick, Doc walked past Jacob and the Doctor as they spoke in low tones into her room, laid down beside her bed. He never left her side.

For months after, Doc would disappear from the farm. Jacob would drive to the graveyard where his folks lay, and he'd find Doc lying on her grave. He'd sit awhile, then headed back to the farm. Doc would show up after a time. He laid down beside Jacob. He even let Jacob pet him sometimes; sometimes, however he was still a hellhound.

R A JACOBSON

His beautiful black wings

CHAPTER 6

THE GROUNDED

Zach's grandpa nailed the owl on the barn door, wings spread. He said it would keep the rodents and crows away.

Zach stood in front of it. He looked at its flat, enormous eyes for a long time. It confused him. How could a creature of such freedom and grace be dead? A being that could defy gravity could look down on clouds, be no longer alive? How could a creature of the air now be on its way to the ground?

Zach had seen death before. Death was just part of life on a working farm. He knew all things began and ended. He had helped when his pa and grandpa would butcher a pig mostly by standing and watching. He watched the blood pool and run across the floor, eventually becoming a sticky mess that blackened. His grandpa hosed the garage floor down, sloshing the blood out into the yard.

He watched his gramma chop the heads off chickens for Thursday's farmer's market. Out behind the house near the woodpile, she would shove them through short lengths of stovepipe, so their heads stuck out. Using grandpa's axe and a stump of firewood, she'd chop off their heads and stack them like cordwood. She was efficient and worked, unhurried. Just one more job to take care of. She probably was planning what she was going to make for supper as she killed.

"Why do you use the stovepipes, Grandma?" he had asked.

"Chickens ain't too bright. Ya cut their heads off, and they suddenly think they can fly. Then ya got blood all over the yard. It's a real bloody mess." She grinned at her joke.

He hated the smell when grandma blanched them. She'd dip them in boiling water to soften the tiny feathers. It smelt of wet dog and shit. It was horrid.

Later, Zach would think about chickens as he helped pluck the feathers off their light bumpy skin. Together they would sit on the back stoop and clean feathers from a dozen chickens. He only managed a couple in the same time it took his grandma to do the rest. What he thought about as his fingers got sore from pulling the little wet feathers, was how chickens were birds. They had wings, big wings, yet they didn't fly. Grandma said that at the end, when they were about to die, they tried to fly. They tried to be birds. To use those wings and leap into the air. To fly! Perhaps to escape their death.

Zach thought about the chickens as he looked at the owl's wings. He studied those wings. He envied the owl with those wings. In his room, he drew wings. He had notebooks full of wings, of men with wings. He had comics about superheroes that flew on great bright white wings.

An idea struck him on the bus ride to school. The plan was to build a flying machine. He skipped the first period and went straight

A SINGLE ROUND

to the library. He searched out every book he could find on flight. There wasn't much. He found a book on Leonardo da Vinci. He had wonderful drawings of flying machines.

He skipped the second period and sat down to work. He copied the drawings into his notebook. By the lunch bell, he had most of the drawings he wanted.

Zach sat in the hallway, eating his sandwich, looking at his drawings. Much of what Leonardo drew and built was beyond him. He had an idea, though. He was sure the feathers had something to do with it. He could build something he was sure would work.

Third and fourth periods went by agonizingly slow. He couldn't concentrate. He kept staring out the window and looking at any passing birds. He watched them fly. They moved with such ease. He loved them. They slid through the air, untouched by gravity. Like Superman or Hawkwind.

Zach wanted to fly.

He sat by the window on the way home. He imagined himself flying alongside the bus, dodging signs, looping around power lines. He had only a 15-minute bus ride to school and an hour ride on a slowly emptying bus in the evening. Zach was the last to be picked up and the last to be dropped off. The driver maintained the same route day in and day out.

Zach was tired as he walked down the lane to his folks' farmhouse. He still had chores to do before supper. In his pocket, a note from Principal Stevens, probably about the missed classes. He was going for a talking to, then of course, he had homework.

It was too late when he got home to put his plan into motion.

Saturday morning, after he finished his chores, he began. In the barn, he found a flattened box from a washing machine his pa had brought home for his ma. He cut two large wings from the cardboard with heavy scissors. He spread them out on the floor and lay down on them. He marked where his hands ended. He threaded two loops of rope for his hands and a longer length to tie around his waist.

Zach put on his wings. They were half again as long as his

arms. He stood, arms stretched out, and admired his wings. They were not done, but they were great. The last part of the wings were the feathers. He had gathered as many chicken feathers as he could find, he went inside and swiped one of his mother's feather pillows. She'd be pissed, but he needed lots of feathers.

He glued and taped the feathers carefully across the inside of the wings, trying to mimic the pattern he had seen on the owl's wings. He turned the wings over and began attaching feathers again, working to match the feather pattern he had seen. It took most of the afternoon, but when his ma called him for supper, they were done. He was very proud of them. They looked right. He'd have to wait till they dried so the test flight would wait till tomorrow. He went inside, happy and tired. Tomorrow promised to be a big day. It was going to be the day he flew.

After supper, Zach sat with his ma and pa and watched the Ed Sullivan Show for an hour. Then he headed for bed where he studied his drawings, thinking about what he built and how cool it was going to be. Tomorrow, tomorrow, he could hardly wait. Sleep didn't come right away. He lay envisioning his first flight. Tomorrow was going to be the start of his new life.

After breakfast, Zach ran through his chores. It was a sunny, warm day. A perfect flying day. He went into the barn. The wings were dry. They were perfect.

He bundled them up in his arms and carried them to the ladder that led to the hayloft. The ladder in the corner of the barn. It was narrow and steep. Just boards nailed to posts on each wall. The opening through the loft floor was going to be tight. He pushed the wings up in front of him. He stood on the first rung and angled the wings till they slid up. He took another step, turned the wings slightly and took another step.

Finally, the wings were through. He held them above his head, then carefully lay them on the straw to his right. He climbed up and into the loft.

It was a huge open room. Light spilled through the spaced boards. The floorboards were nearly entirely covered with straw. In the center of the space was a stack of square bales. They were from last year's harvest, and some had burst. He and his brother played up here a lot. They built forts in the bales. He often came up here to read. It was a safe, warm place to be alone.

At either end were large sliding doors. The one to his right overlooked the yard. It was where the bales were loaded. From the barn's ridge pole hung a pulley. At the end of the rope was a set of metal hooks that grabbed the bales. They always looked like large claws to his mind. They scared him a bit, but he wouldn't let anyone know that. The ground in the yard was hard-packed. It would hurt if his wings didn't work. They'd work no problem, but just in case, he would go out the door at the other side. It overlooked the pigpen. The ground there was mostly mud. Maybe some shit, but definitely soft. He really didn't want to land there. He looked down. It looked higher than he had thought it would. From below, looking up, it hadn't looked high enough. He had never really thought about jumping.

It's kinda high, he thought, shook his head and set his shoulders.

No problem. The wings would work, for sure. He walked back into the barn where he had left the wings. He pulled them onto his shoulders and cinched up the ropes. He slid his hands through the rope loops near the ends of the wings and gripped them tightly. He extended his arms, holding the wings out wide.

Zach felt strong and powerful. He stepped to the loft door. A small wind pushed at his wings, making him step back a pace. He stepped forward and looked down. No, that was a mistake.

"Don't look down." He said to himself.

He looked up across the pasture. Soon he would be soaring over all of this. Soon he would look down on the barn and the farmhouse. It was going to be so cool.

Zach stepped to the edge of the loft door, the toes of his runners overhanging the edge slightly. He stood there. He tested the wings, flapping them experimentally. The wind pushed at them. He shuffled his feet. He looked down. He looked at his wings. He took a pace backwards, stopped, ready.

His heart flew up into his throat, he ran forward, and he leaped, arms out. His fists gripping the rope handles on his wings. As his foot left the barn wood, he arched his back and pushed down on his wings.

For a brief millisecond, he seemed to fly.

He slammed into the ground, his knees buckled, folded, nearly touching his ears. The wind was knocked from his lungs. His feet sunk deep into the ooze and shit. He fell forward, his head and face going into the mud.

He lay, arms splayed, face in the mud, gasping for air he couldn't find. After a long moment, he finally pulled his face free and sucked in a huge gasp. He breathed a few more breaths. The stink hit him. His face was covered in black mud and shit. He looked down, not only his face. Everything was covered. His clothes, his hands and his wings. His beautiful feathered wings were black with crud.

"Fuck." Zach said quietly, kneeling in the muck.

He stood. His legs were sore, especially his left, but nothing was broken. He pulled himself out of the mud, dragging his wings along behind him. He got to the fence and threw his wings over and climbed over. It was then he noticed he had lost one of his shoes.

Zach looked back at the pigpen. He liked those shoes. He climbed back over the fence and made his way back to the spot where he had landed. After a minute of digging, he found his shoe and pulled on it. It took some effort, but it came free with a wet sucking sound.

"What'n'hell, you up to, boy?" His dad came around the barn.

"Nothing," Zach said, standing calf-deep in shit and mud-

A SINGLE ROUND

coated in the stuff, holding one of his shoes. His dad looked at him, with a shake of his head, turned and walked away.

"Don't let yer ma see you like that. She'll have a kitten." He called over his shoulder.

Zach looked down at himself. She would. He'd have to get cleaned up. He walked to the water-trough the cows used and turned on the tap. It was cold. He splashed his face. He pulled his T-shirt off and plunged his head into the water. This was going to take forever.

Zach made up his mind and stepped into the freezing water. He rinsed till he had most of the muck off, then stepped out. He shivered. He was grateful for the sun. He sat and leaned against the fence and looked back where his broken, filthy, crumpled wings lay. They failed. He failed. He had not flown.

Zach sat and thought about flying. He needed a new plan. When his ma stepped out onto the porch and called for supper, he still didn't have a plan. He was at least dry. He stood and walked to the house carrying his still wet shoes.

Zach was running. It was dark. Behind him, he could hear shouting voices, angry voices and the sound of footsteps running after him. They were not far off. If he was going to escape, he would have to lose his pursuers. There just seemed to be so many of them. Another few popped up around every corner.

Zach ran, slipping on morning damp cobblestones. He scrambled around a bend into a dark alley. He pressed his back against the wall. He was out of breath. His heart was racing.

Slowly and cautiously, he leaned around the corner and looked back the way he had come. The street was deserted.

Zach breathed out a breath he had been holding and leaned back.

He stood. He had lost them.

He heard the dogs barking and snarling. He hadn't lost them at all. There were more of them than ever. He turned and ran down the alley. The alley curved to the right. He passed the bend just as the first dog strained at its leash and pulled the soldier behind it.

He glimpsed the soldier. He was dressed all in black. It was a uniform; he knew. It was a Nazi uniform. He was being chased by Nazis.

Everything fell into place. He knew where he was and what was going on. He was in Paris, and he was part of the resistance.

He now knew where he had to go.

He looked up. Over the dark silhouettes of empty buildings, he saw the Eiffel tower. Also, a silhouette against the cloud-streaked sky.

Behind him, dogs barked, and men yelled.

Zach ran.

He knew where he had to get to as if he had been here before. He needed to get to an enormous stone church.

He ran. The dogs barking were closer now. He sprinted around a corner. He could see the church only a few blocks away. Across the street, he could see more men in uniform. He slowed. He kept close to the wall. He crept along. They hadn't seen him yet.

Suddenly an arm grabbed him and pulled him into the shadows. Zach struggled but could not break free. The arm around his neck was strong. Lips against his ear. He could feel the man's breath.

The man whispered. Zach heard but didn't understand.
After a second, the man released him. Zach spun. Immediately he recognized the man. He was a friend. He was one of the resistance.

"Go." The man said.

The Soldiers across the street had seen him. They were yelling and pointing.

Zach turned and ran. Across the cobblestone courtyard and up the stone steps to the large wooden doors. He could hear dogs

A SINGLE ROUND

barking close now, and men shouting. He glanced over his shoulder. They had grabbed the man who had whispered in his ear. Whispered a secret.

Zach raced up the stone steps that spiralled up to the attic. They were close now. Very close.

Zach got to the attic. It was dark.

Narrow planks lay end to end across the rafters. He ran along them. They led to a large round window. It was open. He looked down. It was a long way down. Behind, he heard a splintering sound. He looked behind him. They were coming, and so was something else.

The light coming from the open window spilled into the room but only reached a short way in and made the dark impenetrable. They came out of that black, soldiers struggling to hold massive black furred dogs, but what came behind them froze Zach.

The muzzle of an 88mm gun came into the light first. The black opening so large Zach could have easily put his fist down it. The metal mass of a gigantic Panzer tank rolled forward. The sound of splintering wood as its tracks crushed the rafts. The turret scraped against the ceiling. Bits of wood and plaster fell across the sides of the black tank.

He was trapped. The tank moved steadily forward. Exhaust poured from the side of the tank. The roar of the engine was mixed with the metal clanging of the tracks. He watched as the 88mm cannon slowly turned toward him. He looked wildly about. There was no escape. He looked down, ready to jump and fall. He would smash on the stone steps below.

Zach remembered what the man had whispered. He remembered the secret. He turned to the open window and looked at the clear night sky. He smiled and jumped. The man had whispered the secret of flight.

Zach flew up and away from the window and the heavy tank in the dark. He flew higher until the ground shrank beneath him. He laughed out loud at the joy of flying.

Zach hoped he would remember the secret when he woke.

He didn't. Zach woke to his ma calling him for breakfast. He tried to remember the secret but couldn't. It slipped away from him as dreams are apt to do.

Months later, he was still thinking about flying. His pa had said he could become a pilot, maybe a crop duster.

"They made good money dusting fields," he said practically.

Ya, and they crash a lot and probably get cancer from the pesticides they spray. He thought, but he said nothing. Skimming inches from the top of the fields was not flying. But it didn't hurt to let his pa think it was. It would make it easier to get his pa to agree on lessons.

Zach was old enough, well almost. According to his guidance counsellor, he could get a licence as young as 17. That was a little more than a year away, but the cost was going to be a problem. It was a lot. More than his pa would spring for. Way more. Even if it led to a job, he understood.

He wasn't sure how, but he had to find the money.

At school, his best friend George was sick of hearing about flying, about a pilot license and the money.

"Every fucking day. I'm sick of it!" George lost it, "Why the fuck don't you just go see the Judge and get it done!"

"The Judge?" Zach asked.

"Ya, the fucking Judge. He'll give you whatever you want. All ya gotta do is sign a contract. No biggy." George said.

"What are you talking about?"

"Wait, you don't know about the Judge?"

"Give me a break. What?" Zach asked.

"The Judge. Ya go meet him at the crossroads over on 11, I

A SINGLE ROUND

think, at midnight. He shows up in a sweet ride and gives you what you want."

"Sounds like bull to me." Zach wasn't going to let George trick him.

"Nope. Heard about this kid named Tommy. He did it, but I suppose that didn't go so good. He ended up shooting his head clean off. Another kid I heard about Jacob or something, got a truck."

"Still sounds like bullshit to me," Zach said, but the idea was there in the back of his mind. It was an idea that grew like a weed or thorny vine. Aggressive and tenacious, spreading and twisting into his thoughts, even his dreams.

Soon he was thinking about it almost as much as he thought about flying. Perhaps more.

He questioned George about it, but he didn't seem to know much else. Just the legend, the stories most everyone had heard.

"You know? The Judge. Everyone knows." George said.

"Ok, but where, where's the crossroads? Where do I go if I wanted to meet him?" Zach pressed.

"Well, fuck, I don't know. Somewhere out near that bar outside of town. The Scratch something. It's out on 11. I think it's a biker bar."

"Well, that's no help."

"Ya well, I fucking don't know, do I? You are just as bad with this as you are flying for fuck sake." George said.

Quietly, Zach started asking around. Some kids laughed at him. At first, it bothered him. He already was the weird bird boy. The boy that wanted to fly. Now he was the weird boy that wanted to meet the Devil. And fly.

Zach kept asking.

George and Zach stopped at the gas station on the way home from school to grab a coke. They watched the street. They watched cars drive past, watched them stop and fill up with gas.

It was nice to lean against the coke machine in the shade, drink cokes and watch the world around them.

Rumbling from down the street excited them. Something

different, something new. Bikers. They loved watching bikers. They looked so cool.

George and Zach had often pretended to be bikers riding down the street on their bicycles, often clipping a piece of cardboard to the back wheel brace, so the cardboard clicked against the spokes making an engine sound, but that was last year. Now they were too old for that kind of thing.

Bikers were still cool though, so George tapped Zach on the shoulder, excited. Zach grinned back. They watched as four bikes rolled into sight. In a loose formation, they slowed and pulled into the service station and rolled up to the pumps. The bikes roared once and were quiet. The bikers pushed out the kickstands and tipped their bikes. They stood. All were long and lean with cocky swaggers to their every movement. They looked like outlaw cowboys from the movies Zach liked.

They all wore leather jackets, and denim vests with crests on the back. The crest was of a skull crossed with a hammer and a bearded axe. "'The Jurors'" written in an arch over the skull. Zach thought the skull was cool but didn't understand the name.

George chuckled nervously as two of the bikers walked toward them. George was taller than Zach but avoided any kind of fight. Not that he was a coward; he just didn't like fighting. Zach didn't like fighting, but he would not be intimidated. Even by cool bikers. They sauntered up to the boys who had forgotten they were leaning against the coke machine.

"Hey. Wanna move?" One of the bikers asked and gestured to the machine. The boys jumped as if poked.

"Ya sure... sure, no problem." George stammered. Zach chuckled. They stood back as the bikers laughed. One patted Zach on the shoulder, and they turned to the machine.

"HEY!" One of the bikers called to the biker still at the pumps, filling the bikes with gas.

"You wanna a coke?"

"Naw," he called back.

A SINGLE ROUND

While this was going on, Zach went up to the biker who had patted him on his back.

"Hey, can I ask you…?" he stumbled.

The biker looked down at him.

"What can I do for you, little man?"

"I need to ask.." he trailed off.

"What do you need?" The biker smiled.

Zach straightened and asked, "What do you know about The Judge?"

"The Judge?" He grinned, "Why do you want to know about The Judge?"

"I need his help."

"He doesn't help. He just takes." The biker frowned slightly, "He just takes everything."

"It doesn't matter. I need his help." Zach looked straight into the biker's eyes. He realized suddenly the biker was only a few years older than he was.

"I need to meet him," Zach said.

The biker looked at his friend, now standing next to him. They looked at Zach.

"Yer not going to let this go are ya?"

"No.," Zach said.

"You will regret it no matter what you get, it never will be worth it." He ran his hand through his hair and looked at his friends, now sitting on their bikes waiting for him. He turned to Zach.

"South from 11, on 89 where 89 crosses township 78 bout 6 miles. Go there, just before midnight. He will meet you but make sure this is really what you want. There's no going back."

"Thanks." Zach said, "I know what I want. It'll be worth it."

The biker shrugged and walked back to the bikes, mounted and roared off. Zach watched them.

"It'll be worth it," he said to himself.

The crossroads the biker described was too far, way too far away for them to bike to and explaining to Zach's mom why they needed to ride out to an empty gravel road at midnight would be impossible.

George's birthday was in September, right at the end. He would be 16, and then he could drive. Maybe he could 'borrow' his ma's car and drive them out there, but that was months away. Zach was frustrated. This was the first time someone actually had any real information for him, and he couldn't use it.

It was maddening.

He rode his bike home late that night. It was dark. He had stayed for supper at George's folks' place, which wasn't unusual, but this time riding home in the dark was. It felt so different like he was riding on a stretch of gravel road he had never ridden a hundred times before. Each foot of the road that should have been as familiar as his own home was different somehow, different and slightly sinister.

He rode, looking over his shoulder. He jumped, his head swivelling around at every sound, even the slightest. As he rode, it got darker. Trees looked like they reached for him. Every shadow held a fierce creature lying in wait for him.

By the time he rode up his driveway, he was pedalling as fast as he could. He rode into the farmyard, through the pool of light the yard light cast up to the house. Completely out of breath, he skidded to a stop in front of his house. And looked behind him. It was his farmyard, nothing different, no monsters just about to pounce on him, no demon chasing him.

He smiled and shivered, walked his bike into the garage and went inside.

His pa and little brother were already in their rooms, his ma was watching a movie on TV.

"How was supper?" She asked as he passed.

A SINGLE ROUND

"Good. Goin' to bed. Night."

He went up to his room and shut the door. He plopped down on his bed. He lay thinking about the crossroads. How was he going to get there? He couldn't wait till September. That was too long now that he was committed. Now that flying was possible, really possible if the stories were true. All he had to do was get to the crossroads, and every dream he had ever had was possible.

He lay looking at the ceiling. He glanced at his bedside clock. It was 11:30. He thought about being at the crossroads right about now, just 30 minutes from his dreams. It wasn't fair. Why couldn't the crossroads be closer? Why did it have to be those crossroads? Why couldn't it be any crossroads? He's the Devil, isn't he? Why can't he just go where he wants?

He stood. The end of his lane was a crossroads of sorts. His lane came off township road 18 but on the other side of the road was a trail his pa used to get to the south quarter with his combine, so it was a crossroads. Even he thought it was a long shot, but fuck it, why not? He pulled his runners back on. He heard his ma in the bathroom. The house was dark and quiet, only the small sounds a house makes in the night. He walked carefully down the stairs. He was good at missing the steps that creaked. He found the closer he stepped to the outside of the stair treads, the quieter they stayed.

He walked through the dark house, through the kitchen to the back door. When it was a warm night, the door was usually left open like it was tonight, only the screen door shut. He pushed it open just enough to slide through. He held it and closed it slowly. The spring creaked softly.

He walked across the porch and out across the yard.
Shep, the old German Shepherd, came out of the shadows wagging its tail. She was an old dog with a grey muzzle. She walked with him as he headed to the road.

The dark was heavy around him as he left the yard light's pool of yellowish light. His eyes would get accustomed to it. He felt safer with Shep along. She lived her entire life outdoors and knew when something was about. Together they walked along the drive to 18.

He felt more than saw when he came to the road. It was gravel like his lane, but it was raised from the lane's grade. He stood in the middle of the road and waited.

As his eyes became accustomed to the dark, he started to see. Slowly he could see the horizon where the sky met the fields. It was only slightly lighter. Off to the south, he could see the yard light from George's folks' place. And off to the northeast, the sky had a slight glow. He guessed that would be the city.

Shep lay down by his feet. Zach looked up at the sky. It was littered with hundreds of stars. He could easily see the milky way and the big and little dippers. It was beautiful.

He looked at his watch. Still 15 minutes to midnight. He sat down cross-legged with Shep and looked up at the stars. He lay back on the road, his head against Sheps warm side. He watched the stars, imagining flying up to them. Soaring through space on gigantic bright white wings.

He must have fallen asleep right there in the middle of the road. His body jerked awake. Shep shifted and looked at him. He rubbed his eyes and looked at his watch. It was past 2. He groaned and stood.

"C'mon, Shep. It's not going to work. This isn't the right crossroads."

A quiet sound made him turn, and there was a black car, engine off and a tall man leaning against the fender. The man pushed off the fender and smiled. Zach could see the white teeth, even in the dark.

"Thought I'd let you get a little sleep, son. You seemed very peaceful stretched out with yer dog. It's a nice sight."

"Who are you, Mister?" Zach asked. Beside him, Shep growled low and deep in her throat.

The thin man crouched and looked at Shep.

A SINGLE ROUND

"Now now Shep, isn't it? I don't mean no harm to yer master. You just quiet yerself."

Shep whimpered and went quiet. The thin man stood.

"And you are Zachary Bird." Not a question but a statement, "an' you bin lookin' fer me." He looked at Zach for a second then, with a slight shake of his head, said "I'm The Judge, son. What kin I do ya fer?"

For a minute, Zach looked at him, tongue-tied. He said, "Well, ifin' you are The Judge, I suppose you know why I'm here."

"Ah, A test?" He stepped closer to Zach. "Don't take kindly to tests, son. The question I would be askin' if I was you is, 'why is he here and not at his traditional meetin' spot'."

"Ya, why are you here? I was told that you got a spot out near 89 and 78."

"Yes, I do. That has been my spot for many years, but I find I need to make allowances for the younger clients like yerself. Time's a wastin, and I need to make the deals," he stepped closer to Zach, "So Zach, what is it you want?"

"If you are who you say you are, you already know," Zach said.

"More tests? Really? Let's get this done. Of course, I know what you want. I need you to say it out loud. So shit or git off the pot, boy."

"I want to fly." Zach blurted out.

"Ha, of course, you do. Done." He extended his hand to Zach.

Hesitantly, Zach took his hand, and they shook.

"Good. You have a fine evening, young Zachary."

He turned and walked back to his shiny black car.

When he started it up, the noise was nearly deafening in the still of the rural night. The car roared past, leaving Zach and Shep alone again in the dark, watching the taillights disappear.

Zach stood there for a few minutes. He didn't know what happened next. How was all this going to work? Finally, he headed back to the house. He passed through the yard light and walked up onto the porch. Shep followed, turned and lay down on the mat as Zach opened the kitchen screen door.

Zach walked through the sleeping house up to his room. He had barely lay down when he was asleep.

***

He walked from the kitchen through the screen door. Outside it was bright and sunny. He didn't know where his folks were. Shep was nowhere to be seen. He stood in the yard, wondering where everyone was. Zach looked as a crow flew past him through the yard.

The crow flew very close. He could hear the beat of its wings as they swished through the air.

Zach watched as it flew away.

A realization crept over him. He knew how to fly. Inside him in his head or maybe in his stomach was a muscle, a muscle he could squeeze that would lift him. As soon as he thought that, he squeezed. And just like that, he rose into the air. He was above the treetops. He looked down at his house, at the barn, at the farmyard. He floated.

He felt inside of him around his belly button lines that extended out from him in all directions. He could pull on them and move, following the thread. He grabbed a thread with his new found muscle that led forward. He glided forward. Not flying like Superman, but upright, his feet dangling below him.

The harder he pulled on the thread, the faster he sailed. He couldn't get very high. It felt like he could if he were stronger. He supposed if he flew more, the muscle might get stronger.

He flew over George's farm. There was no one outside. He headed back to his farm.

Below him, running in the field, he saw a pack of coyotes. They followed him, looking up. Yapping as they ran.

He felt the tiredness slide over him. He slowed, stopped. The pack milled around right below him.

A SINGLE ROUND

He felt the muscle weaken. He started to sink.

The coyotes started yelping excitedly.

He sank further. One coyote leaped up, missing Zach's toes by inches.

Zach strained, squeezing hard, his back arched. He continued to sink. He looked down at the yapping coyotes. Their mouths were filled with yellowed teeth. They all started jumping, snapping at his toes.

He strained. The growls below him changed. They lowered, became more guttural.

Zach looked back down. The coyotes were changing. They were growing. Their ears lengthened, and their hackles rose larger and grew spikes. Their tails changed from fur to black leathery skin.

But the teeth were the worst. They grew lengthening horridly till they were as long as a butcher's knife. They growled and snapped, drool splashing around. Their tongues, long and pointed, slid along the massive fangs.

He sank lower. The first of the many claws dug into his calf.

His eyes opened. He lay in his bed, the morning sun coming through his window, and fell on the carpet. He lay for a minute, letting his heart slow.

He didn't feel good. As he thought that, he knew he was going to throw up. He flung the blanket from him and raced out of his room, down the hall to the bathroom.

He made it and threw up violently in the toilet.

"Is that you, Zach?" his mother called from downstairs. Zach moaned but didn't answer.

He sat, his head resting on the edge of the toilet, enjoying the coolness.

Suddenly he threw up again, partially missing the toilet. Fortunately, his stomach was mostly empty, and only clear fluid came flying out.

His ma was there. She helped him up and walked him back to his room and down onto his bed. She put the back of her hand on his forehead.

"Well, you don't have a fever," she sighed. "Ok, just rest. I'll visit you in a bit." She patted him on his head and went back downstairs.

He lay, his stomach hurting. He must have fallen asleep.

The coyotes that were not coyotes were back. They snapped at his feet. He couldn't get away. They clawed at him. They snarled like dogs from hell.

He woke with a start. His stomach felt better. It looked like it was afternoon. He looked at his bedside clock. It was almost 4. He had slept the day away.

He tried to get up. He was weak. He tried again and gave up.

Suddenly he was floating again. Below was water. He was floating over a lake. The water was black and looked cold. He could feel the cold coming up from it, chilling him.

He floated along. Below him, he thought he could see something below the surface. It flashed a darker shape in the dark water.

It burst from the water. In the explosion of spray was one of those dog things, but bigger with even bigger teeth. The teeth sunk into Zach.

Zach's eyes opened. It was morning again. He felt better. His ma and pa were there, looking worried.

Zach looked at them and smiled.

"What..?" Zach said. "What?"

"It's been three days," his pa said.

Zach looked confused.

"Three days? Really?" He was shocked. It didn't feel like it had been that long. He tried to sit up. He was weak. As soon as he got

A SINGLE ROUND

upright, his vision blurred, and blackness crept in from the edges of his sight. He flopped back on his bed and his sight cleared.

"We brought over Granny Duzs to take a look at ya." Zach's ma's voice was gentle. He got worried then. It wasn't like her. He hadn't heard that voice from her often. In fact, he could only think of one other time when pa had found the dog, Tucker, laying on the side of the road. He'd been hit by a truck. The truck had not even slowed, just blasted past.

The dog was still alive as pa carried him down to the barn. Ma was there, carrying pa's 243 Winchester with her. She had seen him walking slow down the drive carrying Tucker and knew what needed to happen next. She spoke with that voice as she handed pa his gun. Zach checked to see if there was a gun in the room. There wasn't. He breathed a sigh of relief.

Granny Duzs wasn't his gran. He had heard of her. When he was younger, the older kids at school used to say she'd ate children and was a witch in league with the Devil just to scare him. Now he knew she was just an old woman that helped out at calvin' and came around when a new baby arrived.

She was a bent-over old woman with long hair in a braid down her back. It was blackish at the tip and greyed until it was pure white at the top of her head. Her small eyes were laced with wrinkles but held a shrewd, knowing look. They lay on Zach under heavy brows.

Zach did not like the look in those eyes.

She moved forward, holding her cane.

"Well, Zachary, let's have a look-see." She smiled. Zach saw she was missing several teeth. He pulled back as a finger bent like a stick poked at him.

Her breath smelled of apples and something else not as nice. He noticed that in the middle of her forehead was a smudge of soot as if a finger had dipped in a fireplace before being drawn down the woman's forehead. It wasn't near Easter when the Catholics all walked around with an ash mark on their foreheads.

This looked different. Zach was sure he had seen theirs were in the shape of a cross. This was just a single line. He stared at it. She noticed and pulled back slightly, that boney finger reached out, and she brushed his hair off his forehead.

"Oh!" she said, pulling back her finger against her chest. "This boy is marked."

"What!?" his dad said.

"OH NO!" His ma grabbed pa by the arm, "What have you done?"

"BOY! WHAT DID YOU DO?" His pa lunged forward past Granny Duzs and grabbed Zach by the shoulders.

Zach stammered, not knowing what was going on. He had forgotten his late night meeting with The Judge. When he remembered, he frowned.

"I... I didn't do nothin." He looked at his pa's eyes. What he saw there scared him. It wasn't angry there; it was fear. His pa shook him again.

"What did you do, boy?" he asked more quietly.

Granny Duzs was busy digging in her bag. She pulled out a candle and several other things. She whispered to ma who left and returned with a basin.

"Bring him over here." Granny Duzs said. Pa looked at her, picked Zach up out of the bed and stood him in the middle of the room beside Granny.

The room felt chilly after the warmth of the bed. Granny got his ma to one side of him and his pa on the other. Together they held a blanket over his head. Granny pulled the small basin ma had brought from the floor. Beside the pot stood a small candle with a wire stand that held an oddly shaped black spoon over the flame. The spoon held what looked like silver grey liquid.

As she lifted the pot, Zach saw it was half full of water. She held it in her left hand above the blanket, right above his head. In her right hand, she held the black spoon. Zach could smell the unmistakable smell of hot iron.

She was mumbling, and her eyes were closed. After a minute,

A SINGLE ROUND

he heard the hiss as the hot tin in the spoon was poured into the water.

Zach looked around, confused.

Granny stepped back. His ma took the blanket from pa and held it in front of her protectively.

Granny continued to mumble as she put the spoon down and looked into the pail of water. After she put the pail down, she reached into the water and pulled out grey lumps of what looked like shiny stones.

She looked at them for several minutes with Zach's ma and pa looking on anxiously.

Finally, she looked up and dropped the silver things onto the floor. They landed with a heavy, dull thud.

"It's a done deal." She looked straight at his ma. "Not ya kin do bout it." She looked straight at his pa.

"It's a done deal. Not ya kin do bout it." She looked at Zach.

"Don't know what yer deal's about, boy. It ain't no good no how. Somethin' in yer body's not taking kindly to it."

She looked at him for a second, she picked up her bag, the spoon and cane and turned and left the room. After a few minutes, Zach heard the back door bang shut.

Zach looked at his pa. His pa looked back, shook his head once, and left.

His ma took him by his shoulders and helped him to his bed. "You get some sleep. We'll talk bout this later."

Zach wanted to remind her he had been sleeping for three days, but he did feel a bit tired, so he didn't say anything.

As she left, she stopped and looked at him before heading downstairs.

When he woke, it was darker in his room. It wasn't night, but no longer morning for sure. He glanced at the clock. Nearly 4. He was hungry. As soon as he had that thought, he realized he wasn't just hungry. He was starving.

He sat up in bed. He was weak but stronger than the last time he had woken.

Suddenly his stomach hurt. It was like a spike had been thrust into his gut. He bent forward and coughed. The cough that came out was unlike any sound he had ever made.

He coughed again, louder and stranger. He fell forward onto the floor on his hands and knees.

It hurt. Everything hurt. He felt like a giant hand was crushing him, squeezing him. He felt pressure on his head. He felt like he was being crushed. He coughed again, and it was even stranger.

He tried to call out. To call for his ma, but he could only make a short, almost barking noise. The pain was everywhere. It became everything. He could no longer think. He got lost in the pain.

Just as quickly as it had come, the pain started to move away, slipping down his back, out his arms, his fingers. He felt the pain slip out of his legs, his toes.

He arched his back. Downstairs, he heard his ma calling.

"What the hell's goin on up there?"

He tried to answer, but he couldn't form the words. He was all right, but there was something. It ; important. He felt better than he had for days, weeks maybe better than he had ever felt. He noticed the window was open. He could smell the air. He could feel the weight of the air. He could taste the air. He hopped up onto the windowsill and looked out across the yard.

It looked different. He couldn't see it, or rather he could see too much of it. He turned his head and looked down.
He saw his ma come into his room. He turned to say something, but what came out wasn't words.

She screamed, turned and ran. He heard her run back downstairs.

He looked back out across the yard. He looked up into the sky. He longed. He stepped closer to the edge of the sill, looking up at the air. Air, he could feel as he had never been able to feel before.

A SINGLE ROUND

Behind him, he could hear his ma pounding up the stairs. He could hear something else—a click.

He turned and looked at the door.

His ma burst into the open door, Pa's gun in her hand. She was shoving a shell into the breach. She was staring at him, her eyes wide with fright.

He tried to tell her everything was ok. She didn't have to be afraid. It came out strange—more of a squawk.

She finally got the gun loaded. She slammed the bolt home and lifted the rifle to her shoulder. She pointed it at him.

What was she doing?

He squawked again; he saw the flash and heard the gun go off. The sound was massive. It filled the small room.

He felt something hit him hard in his chest. He felt the wind leave him. He gasped, trying to find air. His eyes were wide. He was in shock. He couldn't believe what had happened. How could his ma shoot him?

He heard his pa yell from across the yard.

He turned, realizing he was falling, but he couldn't do anything. He felt himself roll toward the open window, then he was through. His mouth worked, trying to pull in air. He looked up to the sky. He looked at his wings as his dying body dragged him to the ground. His beautiful black wings. Wings that seem to stretch forward, trying to reach the sky. With these wings, he could fly. Fly from here and go anywhere he wanted. He could touch the sky. He could defy gravity. If he could just catch his breath.

His body hit the ground.

His pa ran up, looked up at his ma, her head poking out of his bedroom window, gun in her hand. His pa looked down at one of the largest ravens he had ever seen.

"I want to be invisible."

CHAPTER 7

THE DOGWALKER

1
Alison says yes
2
Alfredo disappears
3
Alison doesn't stoop and scoop
4
Alfredo has a plan
5
Misty has a bite
6
The Plan
7
A coffee?
8
The first job
9
The man

1
Alison says yes

When you say yes to walking someone else's dog while they go away, the novelty wears off in an hour. Especially if it's a poorly trained dog. And all small dogs are poorly trained. It's so much easier to pick up the dog than to train the yapping rat.

So, when Alison's friend, her boss, not an actual friend, asked her to look after littlefluffball Misty for a few days, she said she couldn't. But she asked again a week later. She was desperate, and Alison felt trapped, so she said yes. Two days later, little fucktard Misty showed up at her door with a bag of food, a bed and a bag of squeaky toys, very squeaky annoying toys.

Alison pinched out a smile as she watched her friend coo and pet the little flufftard. She even cried. After fifteen minutes, she finally finished and left. Alison looked at Misty, standing at the closed door, whimpering.

Four days. Only four days. It won't be so bad. Alison was sure it would be worse.

It was past 8 pm when Misty shit on the carpet. Alison swore, picked up the dog and went for a walk.

"Let's make this quick," she said to the dog in the elevator.

Outside, it was colder than she had thought it would be. She put the dog down, attached the leash and headed for the park, pulling the dog along.

It was cold enough that she could see her breath. Wasn't winter still months away? Wasn't there supposed to be a spring and a summer in there somewhere? She should be inside, warm in front of the TV, not traipsing around in the cold dark so some little fur bitch could have a piss.

They walked along, crunching on dead, dry leaves that fell last fall. These were just the skeletons of leaves frozen. They crunched like potato chips. She could use a bag of chips. Maybe she'd have one when she got back. Maybe she should head back now. She looked down at Princess Fucktard.

"Just have a fucking piss already." She said to the dog.

A SINGLE ROUND

Alison looked around the park. It was dark, with pools of light spaced evenly along the path. Here and there were other sad, pathetic people attached to these selfish creatures walking around in the cold when, like her, they should be at home warm and comfy watching Netflix.

Alison walked, the dog dragging along behind her. She gave a tug on the leash and felt it give. She turned and looked at the fluffy puff, now not wearing a collar. Alison looked at the leash in her hand, still attached to the collar.

"Can't hurt poor little Misty with a collar that would actually stay on." She said to herself.

She looked at Misty, and that dog looked back.

It ran.

Alison watched it run into the trees.

"Fuck. Now I have to chase it."

Alison stood for a sec, wondering what to do. If she lost the muttfuck, she'd probably lose her job. She ran after the little miss puff ball. She hoped it would get tangled in the brush with its perfectly coiffed fur.

As soon as she entered the trees that lined the path, the darkness became absolute. She stopped, surprised. She looked up. The sky was visible, a deep blue against the black trees.

For the first time, her mind was quiet. No words, no internal dialogue. She paused, looking up at the sky.

To her right, she heard Misty's bark. It snapped her back to attention. She fumbled through her purse till she found her phone and turned on its flashlight. The blackness around her became a wall the flashlight pushed against. She stumbled through the trees. Ahead of her, Misty barked again, further to her right.

Her foot caught on a twig or weed, and she fell. Her head slammed against the ground. Her phone flew from her hand.

She pulled herself up on all fours, stood and picked up her phone. It was easy to find. It glowed, laying in the leaves. She stood, and right in front of her stood a man.

She looked straight in the man's eyes. They were grey and somehow both kind and cruel. He was handsome. Tall and thin with close-cropped hair. He held something in his right hand. It glinted dully. He didn't speak, just looked at her. She stepped back from him. She stumbled and fell back again.

After a pause, she frowned. What was that? Shit, she had fallen again. The man… the man, what man? She frowned. There was a man, wasn't there? She shook her head and chuckled at herself.

"Getting a bit senile already. That's what you get for living alone all these years."

The man forgotten, she stood and brushed at her clothes as she walked toward Misty's barking.

She walked around a large tree, and there was Misty chewing on something. She walked slowly up to Misty, crouching, hands extended to grab the mutt. She leaped forward and grabbed the dog. Misty, so intent on her snack, didn't run.

It was then Alison realized she had lost the leash and collar. She could carry the dog home, but she'd have to buy another leash and collar. How was she going to explain that?

Alison looked down to see what Misty had been chewing on. Holding the dog, she bent forward with her phone flashlight.

The ground was covered with leaves. In the middle of the light from the phone was a small pink spot. She bent closer. With a finger, she pushed the leaves back. She brought the flashlight back around to reveal a man's face, pale in the phone's flashlight. His eyes stared blankly up at her. Bits of leaves stuck to his dry milky eyes. Misty had been gnawing on his nose. Right above his eyes in the middle of his forehead was a neat, small dark hole. She stared for a minute, not realizing what she was seeing. When it hit her, she snapped upright.

"Oh!" She said in a tiny voice.

She turned, grabbed the mutt and hustled down through the trees. She ran all the way home.

A SINGLE ROUND

2
Alfredo disappears

Alfredo hadn't enjoyed high school. It hadn't been a time of magic, nor had it been a time of achievement. Not his glory days. No, he had been an awkward, thin boy that couldn't catch a break. He had dreaded going to school. He had hated the very smell of the place. He hated the cruelty that was an everyday occurrence perpetrated by the 'popular' kids on the less popular. He hated the pecking order like the chickens his father raised. Some chicks were just pecked to death for no good reason, but when one chick started, the rest just joined in. That was high school. He hated the cruel indifference of the teachers, who couldn't be bothered to intervene when someone was being squashed by casual agreement.

He would stay home as often as his mom could be convinced; he wasn't feeling well. He got the reputation of a sickly, frail child, which maybe he was, but more than anything, it was a way to escape the parade of abuse.

It was in the fall of his 12th year that he overheard some boys talking about getting a deal. They spoke in hushed, furtive tones that made him listen harder. He had heard the rumours, the legend of the crossroads. Everyone had. Someone's older brother's friend's sister had gone to the crossroads, and now she had moved to the city and was famous. It was all vague urban legend shit. But he overheard his dad say something, a joke about how maybe it was time he went and made his deal.

His mom hadn't laughed; she had gotten mad as if he were halfway serious as if it were something that was possible but a terrible thing to do.

After that, Alfredo started to actively listen for anything to do with the deal. When you were universally ignored, it was easy to sit and listen to conversations. People didn't feel like they had to guard their conversations from someone who wasn't there. And the more he listened, the more real the whole walk to the crossroads seemed like a thing that was done. The stories he started to put together started to be less a friend of a friend's friend but my neighbour or my brother. They became personal and closer to home. They became possible.

Some kid named Tommy, a few years older than him, had made his deal and ended up shooting himself with a shotgun.

Alfredo had heard about that. It had been in the news. The whole town had been very upset about the whole thing. His parents had been out of town at the time, and this Tommy had taken his dad's shotgun and blew his head off. Alfredo remembered his dad talking about it over dinner one night. He had said he wasn't surprised. Tommy had gone through a hard time with the death of friends and his girlfriend right before graduation in a car wreck.

Alfredo found that getting more information was near impossible. He couldn't find anyone who might actually know any details to talk with him. He needed to know-how, but no one would tell him if they knew.

After several weeks of searching, talking to people who seemed to know, or pretended to know, maybe because they thought it was cool, he was no closer than he was when he started to finding out how you actually went about making a deal.

It was the secret everyone knew, but no one would talk about it.

Frustrated, he took what he knew. You had to go to the crossroads at midnight and wait for a man to show up who would grant you your wish. Where the crossroads were or who would show up or what you had to do, he couldn't find out.

Late on a Wednesday night, Alfredo crept out of the house and headed to a street corner near the center of the town. On the north side, there was a field and a farmyard; on the south side was a garage and an empty lot. It was the only crossroad he could think of. There were intersections everywhere in town, but this seemed the most likely spot. It was the loneliest. He rode his bike to the center of the crossroads and sat down. It was late, nearly midnight.

He hoped no car would come along. He watched his watch as the minute hand moved painfully slowly.

At 5 past, he told himself he'd wait another five minutes then

A SINGLE ROUND

at 20 after he decided he'd wait another 10 minutes before heading home. He was cold, and his ass hurt. The pavement he sat on was unforgiving and sucked the warmth from him. He stood. He had decided. He was being stupid.

Suddenly he was surrounded by blaring light. He felt like a rabbit in the headlights of an on-coming car, unable to move. The car rolled up to him and stopped. The red flashing lights lit on the roof, and a cop stepped out of the vehicle.

Alfredo groaned. He had never gotten in trouble with the law.

"What a stupid thing to get in trouble for. Standing here, waiting for some 'man' to come and give him his wish." he thought.

"You ok, son?" the cop asked as he walked up to Alfredo.

"Yes...Yes Sir." He couldn't help himself. He couldn't get in trouble and be rude.

"Whacah doing out so late? Did you fall?"

"Ya, I jus went for a bike ride, and I fell." He lied.

"Well, it's a might late to be going for a bike ride. What's yer name?"

"Alfredo Barnes."

"You, Frank Barnes' boy?"

"Yes, Sir, that's my dad."

The cop seemed to think a bit, looked down the town's main street to where the only hotel and bar were, then said, "Ok, you get yerself home now." He looked at Alfredo, "Straight home, right?"

"Yessir, straight home. Thank you." Alfredo picked up his bike and pushed it to the side of the road. The cop turned and walked back to his cruiser. After a minute, he shut off the red and blue strobes and drove off slowly down Main Street.

Alfredo watched the car roll away from him. He was excited and breathing hard. That had been intense. That was the closest he had come to being a bad boy, a criminal.

He was about to get on his bike and get home when a black car slid up beside him. It was long and shiny. Its headlights were off. Alfredo could see himself reflected in the glass of the dark window.

The driver's door opened, and a tall man in a grey suit stepped out. Alfredo watched him as he straightened his tie and looked down the road at the police car that was a few blocks away. He smiled as he turned and walked around the front of the car.

"Good evening, young sir."

"Hello." Alfredo didn't know what to say.

"This is a bit unorthodox. Not my usual meeting point, but I heard your call. I must apologize for being tardy. I had a previous appointment. It's a busy evening," The Judge said, looking up at the sky.

"So, what can I do you fer?" he looked straight into Alfredo's eyes.

Suddenly, Alfredo couldn't think. He hadn't thought past finding this man. He had put no thought into what he wanted. His mouth opened, but he couldn't think of a single thing to say.

"I…" Alfredo shut his mouth. What did he want? He wanted not to be noticed. He wanted to be left alone. He wanted to not have to hide from the roving bullies.

"I want to be left alone." Alfredo looked at the man in the fine suit and steel-grey eyes.

"I want to be invisible."

The man looked at him for long enough that Alfredo started to feel very uncomfortable.

"Done," he said finally and extended his hand. Alfredo hesitated, extended his hand and shook it.

"Good evening, Sir." A man said from behind Alfredo. Alfredo spun and stepped backward, bumping into the man in the suit. The man chuckled and gently pushed Alfredo forward. The man in front of him also wore a suit. This one was black and sparkled slightly. It shimmered in an odd way. The man wore a large-brimmed black hat like a cowboy's hat, only with the brim flat it shaded the man's smiling face.

"Mr. Barnes. My name is Mr. June. Your contract is nonstandard. The Judge has waived the 666 clause; however, all other clauses stand."

"Humm, ok." Alfredo did not understand what that meant.

A SINGLE ROUND

As he watched, Mr. June crumpled into flies and vanished. He stood for a second and watched the last of the black flies as they disappeared. He turned and watched the man in the suit, the Judge, climb back into his long black car.

"Have a wonderful evening, my boy," he said. Alfredo watched the car roll slowly away. He shook his head and climbed on his bike and rode home.

The next morning, he went down to breakfast. It was the same chaos as it always was. Everyone rushed to get some breakfast and get out the door to work or school.

After breakfast, he rode his bike to school. It was the same old shit. Nothing had changed. He locked his bike and walked in through the school doors, braced for the onslaught. Sure enough, as soon as he stepped in the hall, he saw James. Fucking James. The ass wipe that was the cruellest being he had ever met.

Alfredo bent his head and prayed to go unnoticed, just this once.

Alfredo kept walking, hoping, eyes averted. He could hear James' voice, loud and angry. He was always angry and laughing. Alfredo hated James' voice, hated his laugh. It would happen now. Any second, James would lunge, laughing. He would swing, and Alfredo would duck or flinch, and James would laugh. He would laugh and call him some dog name. He had a slew of names. It started with Alfie, the dog, then bowwow, dog face. His names were cruel.

Soon now, any second.

Alfredo glanced up and regretted it. He caught James' eyes, James' cruel eyes. The eyes that Alfredo had looked into as they gleamed with pleasure at his pain. The eyes looked directly at him, straight into his eyes as they had so many times, then they slid away. There was no recognition. Those hated eyes passed over him and moved on.

Alfredo walked a few more paces. He stopped and turned. He watched James' back as he walked away. Alfredo couldn't believe it. He stood and stared. After several minutes the bell rang, and he headed to his first class.

A pop quiz, of course, it would be a pop quiz. Mr. Peterson liked his pop quizzes. Alfredo sat at his desk and waited. Mr. Peterson walked down the alley and dropped off the papers. He walked past Alfredo without dropping off his test.

"Mr. Peterson?"

"Huh?" He turned and looked down at Alfredo as though he had never seen him.

"My quiz?" Alfredo held out his hand.

"Oh yes, of course," Mr. Peterson smiled as he handed Alfredo the quiz.

The quiz lasted an hour. Alfredo took the quiz up to the front. Mr. Peterson looked up, confused, smiled and thanked Alfredo. He looked back down at the papers.

"May I go to the washroom?" Alfredo asked. He had a feeling.

Mr. Peterson looked up, surprised.

"Umm ya sure," he smiled and looked back down to his papers. Alfredo waited a second. This was weird.

"Mr. Peterson?" he asked.

"Yes," Mr. Peterson looked up, a frown on his face.

"May I go to the washroom?" Alfredo asked and waited.

"Of course," Mr. Peterson smiled and looked down at his papers.

"Mr. Peterson, May I go to the washroom?"

"Humm...yes,"

Alfredo turned and walked back to his desk. He sat for a few minutes, thinking. He stood and walked up to the front.

"Mr. Peterson?"

Mr. Peterson looked up and smiled," Yes?"

"May I go to the washroom?"

"Humm...Yes," Mr. Peterson said. He looked down at his papers.

Alfredo looked at Mr. Peterson. Could this be 'invisible'? He reached down and swept the quiz papers from Mr. Peterson's desk. He leaped up, looking at Alfredo with anger flaring in his eyes. His

A SINGLE ROUND

chair fell back to the floor. He turned and picked up his chair. He turned back and smiled at Alfredo.

"Oh, shoot! Sorry," Mr. Peterson busied himself, picking up his scattered papers. When he had gathered them in a neat pile, he stood and placed them on the desk. He smiled as he sat down.

"Can I help you?" He asked.

Alfredo smiled," No. No, thank you," Alfredo sat down at his desk. This was interesting. He was going to have to do some experimenting. Mr. Peterson had almost instantly forgotten what happened, and for that matter, had plain forgotten him. Alfredo was invisible, not because people couldn't see him. People could see him; they just forgot he was there.

Laurie Kilbank had sat in the desk behind him for most of grade 12. She was beautiful and arrogant and way out of his league. She also had the largest breasts of anyone in the school. Alfredo stood, turned and looked at her. She looked up, puzzled.

He reached down and grabbed her right breast. Felt its firmness, its heft. Wait, it was too firm; it was fake firmness. It felt wrong. Not that he had held many breasts, well any breasts, but this felt exactly like a large role of sweat socks. She stared at him, horrified, leaped to her feet, screaming. Alfredo released the breast and stepped back.

This was the big test. The nuclear option. She stared at him, and her face went blank, then her face took on that haughty look, and she said, "What?"

He grinned and said, "Nothing."

He turned and left the class. Everything was different. What could he do with this?

For the next couple of hours, he ran amok. He did everything he could think of to do. He walked through classes just to see the confused looks the teachers gave him. He walked into the girl's change room and sat for a time until he got bored. Seeing naked girls was fun and all, but they weren't very sexy. It was just so much like the guy's change room. They ran in, changed and ran out. Not at all like he had so often imagined or had seen in movies. Definitely nothing in slow motion and no long hair flips.

He went straight up to James and punched him full in the face.

James looked stunned, so confused at how his nose was bleeding. He just stood looking stupid. Alfredo laughed until he couldn't. He looked at what he had done and thought it was a stupid thing to do. He didn't regret it; it just was stupid. This was all stupid.

He went home to consider what would be a good use of his new power.

15 years later, he knows his 'gift' is a curse as much as a gift. When no one remembers you, you can't have a relationship. You can't have friends or a job or anything. You can't go to university or college.

It took a while for him to realize that he could control it. Not much, he couldn't stop it, but he could turn it down. It was a decision. He could decide to let someone remember him, at least for a time.

He inadvertently had let his Ma remember him. He was coming home when he did and having her recognize him that helped him finally figure out that it was possible. That he could not be invisible if he wanted to. He just had to decide to, and it helped if he loved the person. Really loved the person. That made it tricky. Very few people fell in that category.

After his ma passed, that category emptied, and he left for the city. He never went back. No reason. There was no one there that remembered him.

At first, he had found it challenging. He had to find ways around his gift. He couldn't get a job, let alone keep one. So he turned to more short-term methods of getting money.

He stole. At first, from people. He would stop them outside of the ATM and demand their cash with vague threats of a gun in his pocket. At first, he was surprised it worked, but it did. They looked at him, assumed he was armed and handed over the cash. They forgot

A SINGLE ROUND

him. They looked confused for a second and headed back into the bank.

For several months he stayed in hotels paying cash and enjoying his days going to the same ATM whenever he needed cash. After a time, he grew bored. He needed something else, but he wasn't sure what that might be.

He was sitting in his hotel room watching tv when an idea came to him. He thought about it and started to smile.

3
Alison doesn't stoop and scoop

Alison woke to Misty barking.

"Shit? Did the fucking dog want to go out again?"

She rolled over and pulled the pillow over her head. She would go back to sleep. It was too early. The fucking dog can wait. She closed her eyes tight and willed herself to go back to sleep. It didn't work. She could still hear the fucking yapping, and visions of piles of shit on her carpet made sleep impossible.

Swearing, she flung the pillow across the room.

"Fuucckk!"

She stood and looked at the floor in her PJ's. Her hair was a rat's nest. She didn't feel like dealing with it now.

She walked from the bedroom to the front room and flared at the dog standing at the door, looking expectant.

She shoved her bare feet into boots, pulled a coat over her pj's and jammed a toque over her rat's nest.

The collar and leash lay in a pile beside the door. She reached down and picked it up. There was something about it. Didn't she lose this when she was in the park? Just before the fucking dog started eating the dead guy's face. The fucking dead guy in the park with a hole in his forehead.

She knew she should call the cops. It was the right thing to do. She'd have to answer questions. She'd waste her whole day.
And there was a man. She surprised herself. Yes, there was a man there. A handsome man with grey eyes.

Maybe she'd just go over to the park with the little fuckpuff and just see. See if the cops were there. Someone else probably already told them, but she should check. She had to walk the puff fuckball, anyway. Might as well be in the park, and maybe she would see the man with grey eyes again. Yes, it was the right thing to do.
She bent down, grasped the white fluff shitball and buckled the collar around it tight. It wasn't going to get away this time.

She walked down the stairs and pushed out into the street, dragging the little white shitstain behind her.

It was quiet. Well, it should be. It was stupid early, and it was Saturday. The dog was pulling more than usual. She looked back at the dog. It was hunkered down, trying to shit as she walked toward it. It had left little shit pellets all along the sidewalk. The humiliation just kept coming. Now she would have to walk back, picking up the little trail of shit. Well, fuck that. The dog finished. She picked it up and left the shit where it lay, walked quickly down the street to the park.
A block away, she knew she wasn't going to be able to get into the park. A cop car was parked sideways across the entrance to the park.

Its lights flashing.

She kept walking, absently putting the dog down. When she got close to the car, a cop came around, holding his arm out.

"The park is closed," he said.

"Why. What's happened?"

"The park is closed for an ongoing investigation," he said.

She looked at him. He was young, blonde and cute. She smiled. He did not smile back. She frowned, looked past him, trying to see what was happening. She turned and walked away, dragging the dog behind her.

She was half a block from her apartment when the dog pulled back and growled. She stopped hand on hip, turned and scowled at the fluff fuck. It looked at her, growling. Now it looked past her. She

A SINGLE ROUND

looked at the dog, looked over her shoulder. A man stood behind her. He was tall and handsome with grey-blue eyes. She stepped back and tripped on the fluff ballbag. Landing heavily on her butt. The leash slipped from her hand, and the shitball puffdemon made a run for it. The man caught the trailing leash before Misty could get very far.

She stood.

"Thank you."

He watched her as he handed her the leash. He watched her eyes to see the moment when he vanished from her memory. She would get a confused look in her eyes, look down, look up and be surprised to see him standing there.

She looked down at her hands, then looked up.

"You were in the park last night."

His mouth dropped open, "I'm sorry What...?"

"In the park...Last night, I saw you."

He didn't know what to say. It had never happened before. He stumbled for words.

"Ah, Yes I was," he looked around quickly, "I had lost my dog as well." He lied.

"Oh, you have a dog," she looked down, disappointed but trying not to show it, failing.

"No, not really. I'm just dog-sitting for a friend. That's why I'm here. I just dropped off the little Mutt."

She looked up and beamed.

"Did you see all the cops in the park?" She asked, "I wonder what happened. "

"Yeah, I did. I donno," he looked again up and down the street. This was the weirdest thing to happen to him in a very long time. It was also the most words he had said to a single person in many years.

"Well, it was nice to meet you again," he smiled and walked past her.

Startled and a bit taken aback, she said, "Yes, nice to see you." to his back as he walked away.

She cursed herself for being lame. What a stupid thing to say.

She turned and headed back to the apartment, dragging the crap puff behind her.

Inside the apartment, she pulled off the toque and looked down at herself.

"Well, no wonder," she said to the empty apartment, " You look like a crazy person."

She could smell shit. She looked down at the white fuff accusingly. It looked back. She realized what had happened. She took off her boot. Yup, she had stepped in dog shit. On both boots.

What kind of an asshole leaves dog shit on the sidewalk for someone to come along and step in it?

She bent and unhooked the dog and carried her boots carefully to the bathroom and rinsed them off in the shower.

4

Alfredo has a plan

It took some time to figure out how he was going to do what he planned to do. More than anything, he had to build up the courage. It was one thing to rob individuals for a few hundred dollars. It was another thing to rob a bank of several thousand.

He spent a couple of days walking around, looking at different banks. He wanted one that had specific physical attributes. He wasn't worried about security cameras. He always looked like a blur or glitch on them. What he wanted was a corner he could walk around so that he was out of sight just for a second.

He chose to rob the bank he had been using for the ATM robberies. He liked the way the bank was laid out. He could walk up to the teller, demand the money. He could turn and walk a couple of steps and be in an office that would hide him from everyone for a second, just long enough to forget him. At least that was the plan.

He walked into the bank and went to the deposit slip table. He stayed there for a second, looking down. He glanced around. It

A SINGLE ROUND

all looked as it had before. He took a deposit slip and wrote in large letters.

"THIS IS A HOLD UP. I HAVE A GUN. PUT ALL YOUR CASH IN THIS BAG."

He got ready to get in line as casual as possible when he realized he hadn't brought a bag. Shit. He went back to the slip counter.

What should he do? His first thought was to crumple up the note and leave while he still could. He could write another note, this time leaving out the bag, but how would he take the money with him?

A woman set down her groceries beside him to write out her deposit slip. Her groceries were in a black reusable bag. He reached down and picked up the bag. The woman looked at him frowning, that puzzled look came over her, and she forgot him and her groceries, which he held.

There wasn't much in the bag, plenty of room for cash.

He turned and got in line. There were two other customers in line. The first was taken away to an office almost right away.

He studied the tellers. There were four working. He guessed he would get the young, clean-shaven man to the far left, which was perfect. It was closer to the office he planned to go into. He checked the office, and his heart sank. There was someone in there working. He thought maybe he should just bail. Come back another time.

"No," he told himself. Stick to the plan. The woman would be surprised at first when he walked in, but it would be fine. She would forget who he was and just look confused for a second. It would be fine.

The spot came open. He walked to the young man and handed him the note. The man smiled at him and looked at the note. The smile vanished. The man looked up at him, then back down quickly. Alfredo handed the man the grocery bag, and the man started filling it with everything in his cash drawer.

The alarm went off almost immediately!

He had forgotten to tell the cashier not to take the bottom bills. They were attached to the alarms.

He turned and walked directly to the office with the woman in it. He sat, even as she stood to see what was happening. She looked at him. He watched the confusion.

"I'm sorry, Sir. What were we discussing?"

He smiled. Outside the office, the security were running around. The grocery bag was sitting on the teller's desk, but he couldn't explain it. He was confused as to why he had been loading a grocery bag with money. He saw the note on his desk.

"I was being robbed," he said, none too sure. "Here is the note."

The guards milled about with guns drawn. The manager was trying to make sense of the whole thing. Followed by two guards, he took the teller, the grocery bag, and the note, walked to the back of the bank and his office.

Alfredo thought it was going to be a bad day for that teller. The woman across from him was still confused. She apologized.

"I'm sorry this bank robbery attempt or whatever has got me all flustered. I cannot remember why we were meeting."

"Oh, not a problem. We were finished anyway." He stood and shook her hand. "Thanks," he turned and left the office.

He began to leave the bank, but he changed his mind and went to the deposit slip counter again. He wrote, "I HAVE A GUN. HAND ME ONLY THE LARGEST BILLS. NO SMALLER THAN TWENTY. DO NOT TAKE THE BOTTOM BILLS. I WILL SHOOT YOU."

He walked up the line and stepped up to a teller. She was small and bright and obviously shaken by what had happened right beside her.

She smiled, a bit shaky.

"How may I help you?"

"What was that all about?" he asked.

"I'm truly not sure."

He read her name tag.

" Well, Sharon. Here is my note. Please be calm." He watched

A SINGLE ROUND

her eyes widen. She took the note, and after reading it, she looked up at him. He smiled. The colour left her face.

"Ask me how I would like the cash," he said in a low tone.

"I...I. I'm sorry... Oh," then louder, "How would you like your cash, sir?"

"Perfect," he smiled. "Please put it in an envelope. Nothing smaller than twenties, please."

"Ah... Yes, of course," he watched her pull money carefully from her cash-drawer then put them in a large envelope. She passed the envelope across to him. He took it.

"Now say 'Have a wonderful day. Come again'." He smiled. She smiled despite herself.

"Have a wonderful day. Please come back again."

"Thank you,' he said. He turned and walked back into the woman's office. She looked up, confused. He sat. The woman hadn't risen. She looked at him without recognition.

"I'm sorry, what were we speaking about?"

There was no alarm. He stood.

"We were finished. Thank you for your time," he said and stepped out of her office. He looked at the teller. She was helping another customer.

He smiled and walked out of the bank. She was going to have a hard time balancing this evening.

After a few weeks, he read about a rash of unexplained robberies in the area. He was sitting in his expensive hotel suite. The more expensive things, the harder it was to pay with cash. Without credit cards or ID, a person didn't exist. If a person didn't exist, they could not really pay for the expensive thing. So, to get around the difficulty, the experience thing became even more costly.

It really didn't matter. He had his system now. He could walk into a bank and walk back out with thousands of dollars, leaving confusion and frustration behind him.

After several months, he got bored. It was too easy, no challenge. He started to take chances. Nothing ever changed. He even got caught, sort of. He had taken the bag of money, and a guard was standing right behind him. When he turned, the guard grabbed his arm, but after a second, he forgot and released him with an apology.

He became convinced he could get away with anything. He looked for opportunities, situations where he could test himself.

Going into secure areas and watching the confusion his presence caused. He always ended up walking out. Forgotten.

He was in a bank downtown to make his usual withdrawal when several men wearing ski masks and brandishing guns rushed in. The guard was knocked down, and the men spread out yelling.

It was just like something out of a movie. It was a situation he had never been in. He looked around, grinning. He was enjoying himself. The novelty was perfect.

There were six armed men spaced around the bank. They told everyone to lie down. He watched with childish glee.

"YOU! GET DOWN NOW!" One of the masked men looked at him.

Alfredo looked back. He saw the man's confusion. The man looked down, then up and yelled, "YOU! GET DOWN NOW!" He turned and looked at the other customers lying on the marble floor. He looked around at his companions, saw Alfredo again.

"HEY, YOU! GET DOWN NOW!"

Alfredo turned and walked into the open office to his right.

"HEY!" The man walked briskly toward the office, slowed, that look in his eyes. He stopped, unsure, he turned and looked at the prone, terrified people.

Alfredo came around behind the thug, tapped him on his shoulder and caught the gun in his left hand. He slammed a large wood and brass award of some kind he had found in the office into the man's teeth. The man dropped as if he were a puppet whose strings were cut and flopped to the ground.

Alfredo turned the gun around absently, noting it was a Makarov 9mm and shot two of the masked men closest to him. Now there were three. Two were in the back with the manager trying to get into the safe deposit vault.

A SINGLE ROUND

The gunfire brought them out yelling, pushing the manager in front of them. Alfredo lay with the other hostages as the men ran in. They looked around, trying to figure out what had happened. They saw Alfredo and forgot him. He stood and moved to a closer spot. All three men reacted by turning towards him, guns at the ready. After a second, they forgot him.

He rose and came closer, and again they reacted; guns ready. He stood still in front of one of the masked men. The gun barrel almost touched his cheek. The man glared at him. That confused look passed over his face.

Alfredo waited till the man looked down and then head-butted him full in the face. His hard bony forehead crushed the man's nose and part of his cheekbone. Alfredo heard the crunch of bone. The man dropped unconscious.

"That was a mistake," Alfredo thought. He'd have a bruise, but it worked.

Alfredo was getting bolder. He stood beside the man as he fell. The other two whirled, guns raised.

For a brief second, Alfredo thought maybe he had pushed this too far. He watched as the men's fingers tightened on their triggers. That confusion passed over them.

Alfredo moved to his right a couple of paces. The masked man watched him, lifted his gun. Alfredo stopped. He watched the gun, imagining the bullets hitting him.

The masked man lowered his gun, his brow furrowed. Alfredo moved again with the same result, only the confusion happened quicker. Whatever made people forget him seemed to be getting faster. Maybe because this man had seen him and forgot him more than once, it was getting easier. Alfredo didn't know. He stepped right up to the man. The masked man looked for the briefest second at Alfredo, then just looked past him as if he wasn't there.

Alfredo stood thinking about this. He reached down and picked up the gun the fallen masked man had dropped, another Makavov 9mm. Gun in hand, he smashed the masked man standing in front of him with its butt.

He dropped.

The last masked man ran to where Alfredo stood still holding the gun.

The man had his gun up but seemed unable to see Alfredo at all. He had become truly invisible.

Alfredo knocked the gun from the man's hand. As he bent to pick it up, Alfredo brought the butt down on his head. The man sprawled on the bank's floor.

He looked around; the hostages seemed as confused as the bank robbers had been. Slowly they stood, unsure of what had happened. They had been sure they were going to be killed. Now, the masked men all lay strewn about, and they could not understand how it had happened.

Alfredo dropped the gun and left the bank. It had been a weird afternoon. He headed back to his hotel suite.

That night, and for several nights afterward, the news on TV was all about the weird robbery that almost took place. It was explained away by experts, each with a theory that they presented as the truth. It made Alfredo chuckle.

One of the facts was that all the dead and injured men had been connected to organized crime and a particular group of Ukrainians. The alleged leader of the group was John Koval. They showed photos of the man on the news. He was a large man with a long, almost sad face.

Alfredo looked at that face, at that man. That man was the man in power. He was a man that made decisions. And that realization gave Alfredo another idea.

5
Misty has a bite

The next morning was pretty much the same as the last. The fucking little fuck had to go again. Alison growled and swore as she put on her boots and coat. Jammed the toque down around her ears and grabbed the leash.

"Ok fucky fuck fuck. Let's get this over with." She yanked the leash around the dog's neck and left the apartment.

As she walked out onto the street, she thought grimly. "Only two more days, and I am free of Little Miss Shitsalot."

She gave a tug on the leash. Sure enough, the dog was shitting again, or at least it was trying to. The dog was hunkered over half walking, half skidding at the end of the taut leash. Alison sighed hugely and rolled her eyes, quickly looking around to see if anyone was watching.

Shit, a lady was standing watering her lawn across the street staring at her. Now she had to actually pick up the shit. She watched the dog, waiting for fuck puff to finish, also waiting for the water lady to go in or at least turn around just long enough for Alison to grab shitmyster and run for it.

Fuck. It looked like the nosy old neighbour wasn't going in anytime soon, so… well shit, it looked like Alison was actually going to have stoop. It's just so fucking unfair. It wasn't her dog. Why should she have to pick up someone else's dog shit even if she was watching the mutt for a few days?

She stood looking at the little pile of turd on the sidewalk between her and the shitter. She waited. The little puff fuck sat and looked back at her. Alison looked over to the neighbour. Yes! Her back was turned. Alison reached down, grabbed the flufffuck and ran.

After a couple of paces, she slowed to a fast walk/half run, still carrying the dog, its little head bouncing.

Glancing over her shoulder to see if the neighbour had turned or had noticed the little pile of turds, she turned a corner and ran straight into the man with grey eyes. She bounced off him and fell heavily on her backside. She grunted. The little puff fuck went flying. She groaned as the fluff fuck took off. She looked up. The grey man had extended his hand to help her up.

"You!"

After a pause, Alfredo said. "Ah...Yes." He was still very unnerved by someone actually recognizing him.

"Can I help you up?"

Alison was still staring at him. She was almost surprised to realize he was offering to help her up. She reached forward and took his hand. She stood.

"Thanks." She looked around. The dreaded puffy was halfway down the block.

"Now I'll have to catch the little...ah..darling," she looked back at him. "Where's your dog?"

"Dog? I don't have a dog."

"Oh. I thought when I saw you in the park the other night I thought you were, like the rest of us all walking your dog. I mean, why else would you be out." She stopped talking when she realized what she had said, but he smiled.

"Well, that night, I did have a dog. I was looking after a friend's mutt for the night."

"Oh ya that's right. You told me that. A friend? Girlfriend?"

"Ha, no, just a friend," he said. "Shouldn't we go after your dog?"

"Shit Ya," she said reluctantly.

She looked down the street. The little white devil hadn't moved too much further down the street. It seemed interested in something.

"Oh, Misty is not my dog. I'm just dog-sitting for my boss."

"I see."

They walked toward the growling fluffshitter.

"I don't even like dogs." She blurted out, bit her lip, waiting to see if he did like dogs, and she had just blown it. He did have such wonderful eyes.

"I have to admit I'm not much of a dog person myself." And he smiled. She smiled back.

They got to where Misty was, and Alison realized it was the scene of her very recent crime. The little shitmachine had come right back to where it had laid down some turds and was gobbling them up.

"Oh, gross! It's eating its own shit." She reached down and grabbed the dog. It looked at her.

"It looks like it's giving you a shit-eating grin," he said, straight-faced.

"Ok, that's terrible. Maybe a little bit funny but very groan-worthy." She giggled under her hand.

"Ha, well, at least you don't have to stoop."

She smiled at him, watching the light playing in his beautiful grey eyes.

6

The Plan

Alfredo spent the next week online studying the Ukrainian mob, especially John Koval. From what he could find out, Koval was the head of an allegedly large crime organization. He couldn't really find out much. Just news reports, and these were more speculation than fact, but he could read between the lines. One of the things he found out was who Koval's right-hand man was. That was who he needed. That was the man he wanted to get to know. His name was Jack Bondar. Bondar would be the man who could make the kind of decisions that Alfredo was interested in.

He found out where their 'clubhouse' was and headed over to set his new plan in motion.

Alfredo had been noticing that the effect, the forgetting, was getting stronger. It happened quicker. The people he met barely had time to even notice him before they forgot him. He thought back to the bank job. Some of those men had seen him but had not even really noticed him. He wondered if it could get any faster. If it did, it would be like he really was invisible.

He walked towards the building that was the clubhouse. It was a large three-story brick building in an area that had been many years ago, the wealthy area. The building looked like a very upscale private home, which it probably had been. There were two men casually hanging out, just leaning against the wall by the door.

Alfredo walked towards them. They saw him and forgot him. He walked past them. He glanced at the closest man. The man looked at Alfredo. His eyes slid off him without even registering Alfredo was there. They were confused by the door that opened and closed. But even that slipped from their minds.

Inside, he stood in the massive hall. It echoed. There was a lot of wood and an old marble floor. The building may have been an old hotel or maybe an upscale apartment building some 40 years ago. It was mostly empty and looked abandoned.

There were a couple of men walking towards the front door.

They walked past him without a glance.

Alfredo walked towards the grand staircase in the middle of the cavernous room.

The sweeping wooden staircase with an ornately carved handrail curved up and to the right dominated the main hall. The handrail was worn down to the raw wood, as were the treads. It had been in use for many years. Alfredo walked up the stairs. When he got to the top, the stairs ended on a large landing with balconies leading off to his right and left; however, right in front of him was an impressive set of wooden double doors.

He stepped forward and pushed the doors open. As he stepped through, several men leaped from where they were seated. Many reached for handguns in holsters under their arms. They paused, then they relaxed when they saw no one standing in the doorway. One of the young men walked over and said something as he shut the door.

Alfredo walked into the room, watching as the men returned to whatever they had been doing before he had opened the doors.

He moved into the room, watching the men. It was apparent who was the boss, the man sitting behind a large wooden desk. At one time, the room was very grand, with wood-panelled walls and heavy, rich, slightly threadbare curtains and carpet.

Alfredo walked to the desk and watched the man, John Koval. He was a powerful-looking man. He was sitting leaning back in a big leather chair reading. He was a man with a broad face, cruel eyes and a hard thin mouth. He wore an expensive three-piece suit with an immaculate white shirt. His tie was loosened. He looked up straight at Alfredo. His eyes slid past him. He looked at the man to his right. Alfredo looked at the man. Alfredo guessed this was Jack Bondar, literally his right-hand man.

Alfredo turned his focus on this man. He was a thin restless man with shrewd quick eyes. He had dark hair, just a touch of grey at his temples. He, too, was dressed in an expensive suit. It was simple and clean looking. His dark tie was knotted. This man was the true power in the room. Alfredo watched. This was the man he needed. Somehow he had to get this man to see him. He needed to get this man to remember him.

He bent forward and looked straight into his eyes. Bondar didn't see Alfredo.

Alfredo straightened.

He hadn't been in a position to get someone to remember him. He paced the room. He looked at the young men, all dressed in bright suits. All were young and all armed.

Bondar stood, said something to Koval, and walked across the room. Alfredo followed. He went out of the room and walked down the hall. At the end of the hall, he turned and pushed through a door. Alfredo followed, pushing the door open before it closed. The door said 'men's'.

The room, like everything here, was tired but still had a certain elegance. The three stalls along the right wall were made of wood with raised panel doors and brass latches. The left wall was four highly detailed ivory pestle sinks, matched with gold faucets and gold-framed mirrors. A window at the end of the room let in dappled light through the trees on the street below.

Bondar walked to the second to last sink and washed his hands.

Alfredo walked toward him, trying to think of a way to get

Bondar to see him. Maybe if he slapped him, he would notice. Alfredo didn't think so, but he would try anything at this point.

Bondar jumped back from the mirror and yanked his gun from under his coat. It was a Makarov 9mm. He aimed two-handed directly at Alfredo, but a confused look crossed his face, and his gun lowered. It snapped up again. A dark look on his face replaced the confused one. He pushed open the nearest stall door, bracing to fire. He moved to the next stall door and the next. He lowered his gun to his side. He looked around the room. He started to put his Makarov back in its holster at the small of his back as he walked back to the sink, shaking his head. A wry smile on his lips.

He had reached the sink. He looked in the mirror and spun the 9mm coming into his hand again, aiming directly at Alfredo. He stood braced, looking around the room, confused. He looked into the mirror and then back to the room, the Makarov up and ready.

Alfredo stepped forward at a pace. Bondar looked in the mirror, tensed, the gun rising a fraction.

"You can see me?" Alfredo said.

Bondar's brow furrowed. His eyes raced around the room. He moved slightly closer to the mirror. He glanced into the mirror.

"Can you see me?" Alfredo asked.

After a hesitation, Bondar said. "Yes, I kan see youu." He looked at the mirror, glancing back at the room, at the ceiling. He crouched quickly and looked under the stalls.

"hwhair r yuu?" Bondar said.

Alfredo laughed. "I'm right beside you." And he was.

Bondar spun to the empty room, then looked back at the mirror where Alfredo was standing right beside him.

"Hwhat's goinkon? Who da fuck r youu? Hwhere da fuck r youu?"

"Can you imagine if I wanted to kill you?"

Bondar pulled back, gun raised, frantically aiming around the room.

"I'm here in the room with you, but you can't see me. No one can. I'm letting you see me."

"Hwhair r youu!" he screamed.

"I'm not here to kill you. I have a proposal for you." Bondar stayed braced and ready, his eyes flashing around the room.

"Jack, relax. I'm not here to kill you. Come here. Look in the mirror so we can talk."

Bondar seemed to get a hold on himself. He lowered the gun slightly and stepped toward the mirror. After another quick glance around the room, he looked at Alfredo in the mirror.

"Hwho r youu?" he asked, working on regaining some of his cool, working on controlling a bizarre situation.

"Well, that's a question. I am someone who has a special condition that makes him uniquely qualified to provide a certain type of service. A service I am certain you need."

"Serrvice? Hwhat youu talkingk about? Hwhat is it you think you know 'bout me?" Bondar's gun was now at his side. He was in a familiar situation in spite of the weirdness of talking to a mirror. He was negotiating. Alfredo was impressed by how fast Bondar reacquired his calm, at least outwardly.

"You are a very bad man. A man who needs the removal of certain obstacles."

"Hwhat youu talkingk about? Speak clearly."

"You need people killed." Alfredo smiled into the mirror at himself, who smiled back.

"Kilt? So youu kill people?" Bondar asked. He realized he still had his Makarov in his hand. He lifted his jacket and tucked the gun away.

"In dat case, den I tink we do business," and he smiled at Alfredo, who smiled back.

7
A coffee?

Alison picked the shit-eating fluff ball up.

"Want to get a coffee?" Alfredo asked.

Alison looked at him.

"Yes, that would be nice. Let me drop off the dog?"

"Sure."

They walked side by side toward Alison's apartment.

Nothing was said. They just walked. Usually this would have made Alison extremely uncomfortable, and she would have filled the awkward silence with a non-stop babble, but here she was completely aware that there was silence and just as aware that she felt it was ok. She had never felt that kind of calm. As she noticed, she started to get nervous. Maybe she was wrong? Perhaps it wasn't comfortable, and she was wrong? A scenario ran through her head, each new wrinkle in her mind adding a new worry until she couldn't stand it. She stopped just feet from her building's door.

She turned to Alfredo and looked up at his grey eyes. Something there stopped whatever she had been about to say. She felt her shoulders slide down from their clenched perch and stared at him, at those calm deep grey eyes, and he leaned forward and took the leash from her hand.

He kissed her.

She stood still, arms at her sides. The noise in her head, that constant chatter she had lived with for her entire life, silenced. She didn't notice until much later. Later she would remember a lot of things, but just then, with her mind blank, she watched his eyes shift through shades of grey, and suddenly they were blue, a blue of ice and summer evening sky. She watched mesmerized.

"Shall we go up?" he asked.

She turned and pulled her keys out. She looked back at him. His blue eyes, they were definitely blue, looked back at her. He smiled.

"Yes?"

"Your eyes?"

"Yes?"

"Were they always blue?"

He smiled.

"Yes," he said. "I have my mother's eyes."

"Oh..." She smiled and walked toward the building; Alfredo walked Misty by his side.

8
The first job

It was a strange conversation. Bondar leaned forward, looking into the mirror, and Alfredo stood behind him. They talked about services and prices and the how and the why of the job Bondar wanted to be done. Alfredo knew it was a test.

Bondar was still unsure, which Alfredo could easily understand. How many times did you have a conversation with a man that only appeared in a mirror? Kind of a reverse vampire.

What Alfredo was confused about was that he could not let Bondar see him except in the mirror. In the past, he had made some people see him, usually only people he loved, but he had worked on it and with brief moments of success. Usually, he used it with hotel clerks or taxi drivers. It made things easier.

As they talked, he tried to let Bondar see him even for a second, but no matter how hard he tried, Bondar could only see him in the mirror. Even that was tenuous. Bondar was squinting and concentrating hard on seeing Alfredo. Occasionally Alfredo would say something, and Bondar would not hear.

Alfredo was getting tired. It was taking more effort than he realized to maintain this connection.

Bondar left and returned in a few minutes, carrying a folder. He laid it down, rifled through the pages, and pulled out a photo of a man. This was to be Alfredo's first job. The payment was substantial.

Alfredo picked up the folder and left.

It was easy. Everything about it, the folder gave details of 'the man'. Alfredo avoided his name. He had read it, of course. However, he put it out of his mind. If he was going to be a contract killer, he didn't want the ghosts of his jobs to have names. Somehow it made him feel better to not be able to name the men he would kill.

'The man' had a fairly consistent routine. Alfredo acquired a gun and silencer.

On a chilly evening, he walked into the park where 'the man' walked his dog at 9 pm. It was simple to step up to 'the man,' lift his gun and pull the trigger.

Alfredo watched the man topple backward with a perfect little hole in his forehead. He landed on the dry leaves. They jumped up all around 'the man,' and they half-covered him when they fell back down.

Alfredo stood for a second, looking down at his job. He turned to see a small dog come running out of the trees, followed by a very pretty girl.

She fell, stood and saw Alfredo. She would forget him. Everyone did. It was just a second away. He turned and left the park, his job done.

9
The man

Together they walked into Alison's building. They smiled at each other. Each aware that something had passed between them. Each determined to remember every second of this beginning. They each knew it was a beginning. A beginning of something profound, something unique. An equation that had finally found its true answer. In the elevator, they kissed again. Alison lost all thoughts except for this man and his blue eyes.

The elevator opened. They held hands, looking at each other. Misty pulled back away from Alison's door. They did not notice.
A man stood waiting for them. He was a tall, thin man in a dark suit

A SINGLE ROUND

and a large-brimmed hat. He was smiling. His teeth glowed in the dim hallway.

"Ah, Mr. Barnes. I hope you are well. My name is Mr. August." He looked down at a black leather book in his hand, "I am here to inform you that your contract is no longer valid and has been revoked."

"I...I don't understand. I made a deal. I have a deal. It can't just be revoked." Alfredo looked at Alison. She looked back, confused.

"Yes, Mr. Barnes. You had a deal. There are some irregularities with several contracts, and yours HAS been revoked." He smiled even more broadly. "Have a wonderful afternoon."

Mr. August's head fell forward, his body suddenly jerked back. It vibrated, and the surface writhed with small movements. His head came up slightly. His body seemed to shift, to lose solidity. It fell forward without really hitting the ground. Instead, it disintegrated into a black mass. A mass that writhed and squirmed and thousands of flies burst from the pile. They swarmed forward and around Alfredo, then they dropped until they lay littering the hallway.

Alfredo looked at the dying flies that scattered about the floor. He stood still frozen, looking at what had been a man. He reached back for Alison's hand, "Come on, Let's go in."
But she pulled her hand back, "What's going on? What the Hell is going on?"

"It's nothing. I'll explain. Let's just get out of the hall." He reached for her hand, but she pulled back. She saw that Alfredo held Misty's leash.

"Who the fuck are you, and why are you holding my dog's leash?" Alison's voice rose to a hyper pitch as fear and anger struggled for control.

Alfredo looked at her, confused. He looked down at his hand and back at the dog. Slowly, he handed her the leash.

"I don't understand. I thought…"

"What did you think? Who the Hell are you? Why are you in my building?"

"I.." He looked at her, into her eyes that moments ago had

held something. Love? Maybe or the promise of it. But now, not a hint of recognition in her eyes. "I'm Alfredo," he said quietly.

"I don't know you. Get the fuck out of here, or I'm going to call the cops." Her eyes blazed with anger.

He moved a step toward her, arms coming up. Her eyes widened, flooded with fear.

"NO! Stay back!"

He stopped. His arms sank to his sides. He turned and walked to the stairs. Behind him, he heard Alison scrambling to get her keys out and into the lock. He pushed open the door and walked down the stairs and out of the building into the street.

Once on the street, he started walking with no destination in mind. What did it mean that his contract was revoked? What would that change? Was his soul still The Judges?

He walked his head down. When he looked up, he was in the park standing in front of the spot where he had left 'the man'. He hadn't noticed when he passed the yellow police tape. There was no one guarding the site. He looked around him, then down at the pile of leaves.

He stood still. The park came to life with people walking their dogs. He watched them walk. A hand grasped his shoulder.

It was a young cop, and he was talking to him. He was angry. He was talking to his radio on his shoulder, then back at Alfredo.

Alfredo looked at him, not understanding. He couldn't hear anything. It was quiet. He looked at the cop calmly.

Suddenly everything cleared the cold night air, the park noises and the cop's angry voice.

Alfredo looked at the cop. Looked into his eyes. He waited for the confusion. He waited to be forgotten. The cop kept yelling. He pulled at Alfredo's arm, but he wasn't forgetting him.

Alfredo looked around as the cop led him back across the yellow tape. People with dogs looked at him. They saw him.

They saw him! The realization shocked him. He looked at the eyes around him. They saw him and remembered him.

He yanked his arm free and ran. Behind, he could hear the

A SINGLE ROUND

cop yelling for him to stop. He kept running. Everywhere there were eyes that saw him. He was seen for the first time. There was nowhere to hide.

He slowed. Something was wrong. It was quiet, very quiet. He looked at the eyes around him. He stopped. There was heat, a bright white burning in his stomach. His shirt was wet with sweat. He touched his stomach. He felt the wetness. He lifted his hand up. His fingers glistened darkly.

Suddenly he was sitting. His leg splayed out in front of him. He frowned, not knowing how he got there.

Around Alfredo, people looked at him. He watched them. He was cold. His head rolled forward onto his chest. He was no longer cold. He was sleepy.

He wondered what Hell was going to be like.

He had a smile you could blind yourself looking at

A SINGLE ROUND

Chapter 8

THE RIDE

The sound of air brakes was the the sweetest sound he had heard in a long time.

The hitchhiker hadn't seen a car or truck for almost two hours, so when the lights of a rig topped the hill, he leaped to his feet. It had started to rain an hour ago, and he knew he had miles to go before he got to a town. The highway he was on wasn't used as much as it once had been. He was on the old highway, a two-lane blacktop that serviced the small towns and villages that had been missed when a four-lane had been put in a few years ago.

The rig slowed and bounced slightly as it pulled to a stop beside the hitchhiker.

The young hitchhiker stepped up and pulled the door open.

He pushed his backpack and guitar case up in front of him. The driver was a big man with massive arms, neck and shoulders. He took the guitar case and backpack and pushed them into the berth behind.

The hitchhiker pulled himself up into the seat. He almost groaned with relief in the warmth of the cab. He was pale, almost white, with long dark hair plastered to his head.

The driver held out his hand. "Gordon," he said.

The hitchhiker took the huge hand, shook it once and said, "Steven. Thanks for stopping."

"Almost didn't. I thought you were an animal or a pile of trash 'till you stood."

Gordon pushed the rig into gear and concentrated on getting up to speed. Once they got moving, he reached behind his seat and pulled out a roll of paper towels.

"Here, ya go. Ya, look half drown." Gordon handed the towels to Steven.

"Yeah, thanks," he said and started drying his hair.

"Where ya headed?" Gordon asked.

After a long pause, Steven said, "Just going to meet someone."

Gordon watched the kid dry his hair. He had a haunted look, as though he had been living rough for a while. His clothes, jeans, t-shirt and a light jacket, were dirty and worn. His eyes had a brightness somewhere between near-madness and fear. He was very pale.

"You bin on the road awhile?" Gordon asked.

"Yeah, couple of months," Steven said, his reflection looked back at him. Outside, the dark landscape passed by.

"My folks died in a wreck. I need to find out why." His tone was flat as if he was talking about the weather.

"I'm sorry to hear. What do you mean, find out 'why'?"

Steven looked at Gordon.

"Ah, it's nothin'. Just gotta check something."

It was quiet for a time. The kid's wet clothing gave off a slight animal smell.

"I'm gonna be making a stop in 'bout an hour." Gordon said.

"It's my usual stop for some grub. Good place called The Ol' Scratch Tavern. Food's decent, better than decent. Frank flips a mean burger. It's a bit rowdy, but good folks."

"Yeah, I'm gonna be late if I don't press on."

"Yer meeting is tonight?" Gordon glanced at the dash clock. It was well past 10. The kid followed his look and frowned. It was obvious the math didn't add up.

"I guess I won't make it tonight," Steven said more to himself than to Gordon.

"Well, in that case, let me buy you a burger."

"Naw, I got money. Let me buy you one for picking me up."

"You sure?"

"Yeah, for sure. No problem. I guess I got to find a place to crash tonight."

"Ol' Scratch rents rooms. Nuthin fancy, but clean."

"Perfect."

They were quiet for a few miles.

"Who ya meeting if ya don't mind me askin'."

Steven looked at the trucker for a long time. "Calls himself The Judge. Don't know his real name."

He watched as Gordon stared at him. Steven looked back at the road, and the pools of light the rig's headlights cast.

"Ya I heard ah him." Gordon watched the lines on the road. "It's none of my business, but it ain't a good thing ya go meetin' The Judge."

"Yeah, it's none of your business," Steven replied quietly.

Gordon shrugged. He knew that mindset. He had seen it before. People that were dead-set on seeing the Judge had that look. They weren't going to be persuaded.

After a little more than a half-hour, lights appeared in the distance. Bright pink, white and red neon washed the sky in crimson.

As they got closer, 'Ol' Scratch Tavern' could be read in huge glowing letters. And a depiction of a pointy tailed devil threatening a bikini-clad woman.

Gordon grinned. Seeing that sign, ugly as it was—told him he was going to have a good meal with good people. He glanced over at his hitchhiker.

The neon turned his pale skin a sickly red, which when mixed with the greenish dashboard lights, made him look ghastly, almost ghoulish.

The Ol' Scratch had a large gravel parking lot west of the building. Gordon geared down and rolled into the parking lot. The area closest to the blacktop had a section that was generally reserved for semis. It was open even though the rest of the parking lot was packed.

Gordon eased the rig in and shut her down. He turned to Steven.

"Coming?"

Resigned, Steven said, "Yeah, sure."

Gordon climbed down, a smile on his face. The parking lot was a good indication of what was happening in the bar. It was going to be packed. Gordon loved it that way. After spending so many hours on the road alone, it was fantastic to be with people. Together they crunched across the gravel parking lot. It was full of mostly pickups with a couple of tired beat down cars scattered about. The neon glinted off chrome and paint, making even the tired old cars look good.

Off to the south of the building, where the neon didn't touch, were parked a bunch of bikes. No cruisers, all customs, choppers, bobbers, mostly apes, some low-slung belly draggers, all Harleys. A few Knuckleheads, but mostly pan heads.

Steven's dad had been a rider, sort of and had owned several Harleys. He and his father had fun looking at bikes. His dad seemed to buy a new one every year, all customs. Steven always went along.

He knew this was an unusually impressive collection of bikes, and he paused to look at them. Gordon followed his eyes.

"Ya, that would be The Jurors bikes. A couple of the members are fine custom bike builders. The bobber over there is Jacob's." Gordon pointed to the right at a nice vintage-looking bike, "If you want to talk to The Judge, you should talk to Jacob. They're all marked, but Jacob is their leader if there really is a leader."

"Marked?" Steven looked back at Gordon.

"Yeah, they've all made a deal with The Judge."

Steven looked up sharply. "They've sold their souls?"

"Ya," Gordon shrugged, turned and headed for the door.

"What for?"

"Ha, who knows? Various things, but it's not like I know 'em personal like. Just know that they are marked. It's why the club name. Kinda ah joke, ya know. The Jurors."

Steven caught up and grabbed the door as Gordon walked through.

The bar was loud. It staggered Steven just how loud it was. Out in the parking lot, it had been a low, consistent hum, he had heard but, after riding in the semi's cab, had seemed quiet. Steven stared about the dark room. Everywhere he looked, were people, mostly men, laughing, talking, shouting. There was so much movement it sort of blended into a writhing mass. He stood still, just watching when he heard over the clamour, a sharp, high-pitched whistle. The sound brought him from his trance.

He looked to his right and saw Gordon waving him to follow. He moved forward, holding his guitar case in front of himself, trying not to jostle anyone. He got up behind Gordon and followed closely, moving in his wake. The big trucker made a large path through the crowd without pushing or shoving. The crowd just moved out of his way. Steven was grateful when they made it to the bar. He placed the guitar case up against the bar and pulled off his backpack, lowering it to the floor beside the case.

Gordon had found a couple of chairs not side by side, but a brief conversation got the guy sitting in one stool to move over so they could sit down elbow to elbow. They sat, Steven, looking around, still slightly mesmerized by the scene.

Gordon laughed and clapped him on the back.

"Ya it sumpin', ain't it" Gordon looked over the bar.

"Mostly farmers and some fellars from the plant south ah here." Gordon saw The Jurors off in a corner near the pool table. He pointed. "There's The Jurors over there."

Steven looked where Gordon was pointing. "Holy fuck!" Steven said, looking at the biggest man he had ever seen.

Gordon laughed, "Ah ya, that's Brian. He's one big mother fucker for sure. Heard tell he sold his soul to be invincible, but it turned out everything that hurts him just makes his body compensate by getting bigger and stronger. He also gets dumber as well. Kinda ah cliché, but I guess the Judge has a sense of humour."

The bartender arrived. He was an older man with an unshaven face and a weary look in his eyes. They darted about the bar, seemingly to see everything. Arms wide, his hands flat on the bar, he leaned forward and nodded.

"Hey, Frank. A couple ah beers an' a couple of yer burgers." Frank smiled and did not even try to talk over the noise.

Steven was still watching The Jurors. He leaned over to Gordon's ear, "Which one is Jacob?"

Gordon looked at Steven with a frown and looked over the heads toward the corner. After a second, he leaned toward Steven.

"See the big guy with a big grey beard sitting over in the corner?'

"Ya."

"That's Jacob. But best ya don't bug him now. Best wait till things quiet, a bit." Gordon turned back to the bar as their beers arrived. Steven stared at Jacob. He sat leaning back against the wall, a beer in one hand, a pool cue in the other. He was a large man, lean with muscular arms. He sat with a confident, quiet stillness—a small grin playing on his lips. The ball cap he wore shaded his eyes. There was a sparse wolf quality to him.

Gordon patted Steven on his back, and he turned to the bar.

The pint looked good. Steven picked it up. They touched glasses, and Steven pulled at the beer. God, it tasted good. He hadn't had a beer or much of anything for several days. Now here and now, this beer tasted just about as good as a beer ever does. He looked at the smiling face of Gordon.

"Good?" Gordon asked.

"Damn right." Steven took another swallow. He felt himself relax more than he expected to. He looked up into the mirrors behind the bottles and watched the bar.

The Jurors kept to the corner around the pool tables. No one approached; no one even looked in their direction. Gordon was right. They all looked to Jacob as the leader, even though Jacob didn't seem to notice. He sat back, drinking his beer and enjoying himself. He had relinquished his cue. If Jacob was the leader, then Brian was his second.

Brian laughed and joked in the center of them all. A giant of a man obviously loved by them. Steven shook his head. Brian was the largest man he had ever seen. More massive than any bodybuilder or powerlifter he had ever seen on tv. He towered over them all and yet seemed almost gentle.

Steven noticed something odd. The Jurors never called the waitress over to order. She just arrived with a tray of beers. At first, he thought they had a running tab, but after every round was delivered, The Jurors all took their beers, turned to another table in the bar and raised a toast to the table. The table returned the salute.

The bar was taking turns buying the Jurors rounds. Table after table sent rounds over to them. It was respect. It wasn't fear that kept the patrons from approaching the Jurors. It was respect. The entire bar was paying tribute to the Jurors.

"Now that's interesting. So what does the town think of the Judge?" Steven thought.

The burgers arrived. He looked down.

It did look like a good burger. It looked like a burger a close friend would que up for him on a Saturday afternoon. Big and meaty. It was called the Hades burger. Steven looked up at the chalkboard with the menu written there. Everything was named after something to do with the devil or hell. It was, Steven thought, a bit obvious.

He took a swallow of beer and started in on his burger. It was good, very good. Gordon was already nearly finished. He seemed to be really enjoying himself. The big man hunched over, elbows on the bar, both hands wrapped around the burger as he attacked it. And he was looking around, enjoying the surrounding cacophony.

Steven smiled. This was nice. He was right. Good food, good people.

He was halfway through his burger when he realized, mixed in with all the laughing and talking, was music, not canned music, but a band. He put his burger down and slid off the barstool and started making his way deeper into the bar. Where the long wooden bar ended, the room turned and expanded, and there was a much larger room with a stage, and a three-piece was doing its best to be a little band from Texas. They had just rolled into their version of 'La Grange', and Steven felt his face split into a grin. They were pretty good. They even had beards not as long but still. He suddenly felt lighter than he had for weeks, months. He stood and wished he had brought his beer.

The band had finished 'La Grange' and had started 'Tush' when a voice beside him said. "I fucking love this song."

Steven looked to the sound of the voice. It was Jacob standing beside him, smiling at the band.

"Yeah, me too. My all-time favourite band," he said suddenly, not listening, "You're Jacob."

Jacob paused, the beer almost at his lips. He took a swallow, "Ya." He looked at Steven. "And you are?"

"Ah... Steven." he stuck out his hand awkwardly.

Jacob looked at it, ignored it, and looked up. "So 'Ahsteven,' how is it that you know my name?"

"I hitched in with Gordon."

Jacob looked back to where Gordon could just be seen, burger finished and fresh beer in hand. Jacob looked back at Steven.

"I need to speak to the Judge. I need to ask him a question,"

A SINGLE ROUND

Steven said. He had yelled it just as the music paused. He looked around. Everyone close enough to have heard was looking at him.

"Not something you should be yelling in a bar where you aren't known." Jacob turned and started walking away.

"Jacob I...I need.."

Jacob stopped, turned and looked back at Steven.

Everyone near was very purposely not looking at the two men.

"You can't talk to the Judge. He's not the talkin sort. He just takes what he wants and gives nothing back. Leave him alone. He's not the answer."

"But he killed my parents, and I want to find out why."

"He killed a lot of folks round and worse than that. He has a lot to answer for, but you're not the one." Jacob looked at the beer in his hand. "Sorry 'bout yer folks," and he turned and walked away.

Steven made to follow when a big hand fell on his shoulder.

"That's it, kid. Leave it be." Gordon said, pushing a beer into Steven's hand. "I've seen Jacob get mean."

"I'm not afraid of him." Steven was cocked up, ready to take on the world.

"Ya, well...I am," Gordon said, pulling Steven with him. "And you should be. C'mon I spoke to Frank. He has a room for you. Get yer gear, and someone will show you yer room."

"I just need him to tell me where I can find the Judge."

"Well, maybe Frank knows; he seems to know pretty much everything that's going on 'round here."

They sat down on the stools. Drinking their beer and watching the crowd. It was getting close to midnight, and the bar was starting to empty out.

Later that morning, Steven lay in the dark in his rented room. He wasn't sleeping. He was thinking. Outside his window, he heard The Jurors kick their bikes to life and rumble away into the night.

Jacob knew. Jacob knew how to talk to the Judge. He knew. Steven was sure. But he was also sure he wasn't going to tell him. All The Jurors knew, but without Jacob's OK, they wouldn't talk either.

Gordon was off making his drive. He said he would be coming back through in a day or two if Steven needed a ride out.

"Fuck it," he wasn't going to get any sleep, he thought. He pushed out of bed and flipped the light on.

He stood in the middle of the plain room, not sure what to do. He bent over and opened his guitar case. He looked down at the prize. His dad had come back with it a long time ago, right about the time his business started to take off. Now, looking back; Steven could not figure how his dad could have afforded a guitar like this. It was a Kalamazooo KG-14 flat-top guitar, and it was beautiful. Steven didn't play guitar, but he could see, even feel, this was a special guitar.

He knew about guitars just like he knew about bikes because his dad knew about bikes and guitars. He had never ridden, nor had he ever played. Nor had his dad.

His dad had fine bikes and guitars. Many of them. He felt it gave him an air of rough-edged mystery. He thought it romantic to tell a story of rags to riches. From a guitar-playing bike riding streetwise kid to a high-powered money executive.

It was all a facade—a story he fabricated and maintained. Steven hated his dad for it. That and so much more, but he never wanted him dead. He missed his mom. She was sweet. She didn't care about all the money. She was just a farm girl who fell in love with an ambitious man.

He loved her quaint stories of growing up on the farm. It had become part of the family legend, part of the myth. She told her stories, but one caught his attention more than the others. The one about the crossroads and the Judge. He really liked that one. Asked to hear it again and again. Steven's mom laughed about it at first, then found it frustrating. It started to worry her.

Just after Steven's 12th birthday, his dad's business started to do well. Very well. He had come back from one of his many business trips. He had always gone on several trips a year. After one trip, everything changed. Suddenly things were great. They had everything they ever wanted, and Steven's mom forgot about her worries about the Judge and the crossroads. Steven's father never went on another business trip. A year later, they had a baby, and Steven had a sister.

Her name was Laura, and Steven loved her. Most of his friends hated their little sisters or little brothers. They were annoying and always around, but Steven liked Laura. She was easy and friendly. She was fun to be around. He loved being a big brother. He loved taking care of her.

When his parents needed him to sit so they could go out, he was happy to look after her.

When Laura was 5, she started school at the same school Steven was at. He was so excited. On her first day, he walked her to school and showed her around. It was his last year, and he wanted her to feel safe. He met her at lunch and sat with her. Some of his friends from the art club sat with them and were nice to her. They talked about the yearbook they all were helping design. It was exciting.

After school, he walked her home. Their mom was waiting. Laura ran from Steven's side, telling her mom all about her day. Her mom smiled and looked at Steven.

"Thank you, Steven," She said.

"No problem. It was fun. I have to go back to the school. We're working on the yearbook with Mr. Sauvé."

"Dad was going to take us all out for dinner to celebrate Laura's first day," his mom objected.

"Ugg, I would love to, but I can't. Not tonight."

"OK. When will you be home?"

"8? Probably."

"K,"

Steven kissed his mom's cheek, patted Laura's head, smiled at her and started walking back to school.

It was the last time he saw her alive. He missed her most of all.

The next morning he packed his backpack and went into the bar. It looked surprisingly different. It still stunk of beer, but the tables had been moved around. There were several tables full of people eating. Some had full tables, a couple had singles.

Frank was there serving with a couple of waitresses helping out.

Frank saw Steven. He lifted his chin in recognition. He gestured to an empty table. Steven nodded and walked over, setting his guitar case and backpack on the floor beside the table. He sat just as a pretty waitress stopped by his table.

"My name is Brandi. Coffee to start?"

Steven looked up, "Yes," he stammered, feeling like a small boy.

"Coming right up, hun," she smiled and turned to the table to Steven's right.

"The usual, Billy?"

"Yup, thanks."

"You got it, sweetie."

She walked off. Several eyes followed her every step.

Steven leaned back and looked at the chalkboard menu.

The devil theme continued. The 'hell-of-a-breakfast' looked like a shit ton of food, the 'Brimstone toast,' toast with avocado and spicy jelly. Looked more like what he needed. Devilled eggs, Purgatory poached eggs, Netherworld quesadilla, all served with a Bottomless Pit of coffee.

A SINGLE ROUND

Steven chuckled. He looked up when Brandi put his coffee down in front of him.

"Know what you want, hun?"

"Yeah, the Brimstone toast."

"Ok, hun."

She smiled and turned to Billy.

"Just a sec on your Hella, Billy."

He nodded. Steven watched him as Brandi walked away. Billy was staring at his phone; absently, he looked to the floor beside him. He swore then reached down and picked up a twenty from the floor.

"Fuck," he said, then softer "fuck." He looked up and caught Steven's eyes.

"My lucky day," he said, but he didn't sound happy about it.

"That's great," Steven said.

"Just great," Billy frowned.

Brandi returned with a huge plate piled high with food. Three eggs, two pancakes, three strips of bacon, two sausages, orange juice, toast and of course, the bottomless pit of coffee.

"That's a big breakfast," Steven said.

Billy grinned, "yup," and he dug in with gusto.

After a few minutes, Steven's food arrived. Billy looked up, "That don't look like enough breakfast."

"Yeah, it's enough."

Billy turned back to his plate. He was plowing through it in a hurry.

"Listen," Billy said. "If things er tight, I'll spring for yer breakfast. I jus found a twenty." He grinned.

"No, I'm good. Thank you, though."

Billy grunted and returned to his food. Steven thought for a second. Gordon has been right, good food, good people.

Steven ate his toast, enjoying it. The coffee was excellent too. When he finished, he leaned back. Billy was finished as well.

"Well, 'bout time fer a nap." Billy stretched. "Where you headed?"

"Nowhere special. I got some business 'round here. After, I don't know."

Billy took a sip of coffee and looked at Steven.

"Yer not fixin' to go see The Judge, are ya?"

Steven looked at Billy, then down at his empty plate.

"What if I was?"

Billy nodded to himself as if he had known it. "Ya, you have that look."

He looked at Steven. "I'm pretty sure I can't change yer mind, but I won't sleep so good if I didn't try."

"It's not what you think. I'm not here to make a deal. I'm here to return something to the Judge. I don't want it. It wasn't my deal. It was my dad's."

"Yer dad's, eh?" Billy seemed to think for a minute.

"It don't matter. You go see him, and your life is done. It don't matter what you think you came to do. He will twist it into your worst nightmare. It's what he does." Billy shook his head.

"You seem to know a lot about this," Steven said.

"Ya well, I was a fucking fool. I made my deal, and now I'm cursed."

"So you sold your soul?"

"Ya I did." Billy looked down, embarrassed. "An fer no good reason. I wanted to be lucky. I figured it was safe, I mean, how could that turn bad. Ha, I was so wrong."

"Lucky?"

"Ya. I'm lucky, alright. The trouble is no matter what I win, someone I know gets unlucky to the same amount. It's a balance thing, I was told. I think it was just The Judge likes fucking with people." Billy's voice was heavy with bitterness.

"Well, I'm not here to make a deal. I just want an answer to a question."

"Well, I heard tell that Jacob tried damn hard to get some answers but didn't get anywhere."

A SINGLE ROUND

"Yeah, I tried to talk to Jacob last night. He seemed less than talkative."

"Ya Jacob ain't a talkative kinda guy. He has a serious hate on for the Judge, but he won't talk to no one. Not even me an we're sorta friends."

Steven watched Billy. They both took a sip of coffee.

"I just need to know where to meet him."

"Look, you're not hearing me. Don't do this. It won't work. You won't get what you want."

"I need to find out why."

"Why? Why what?"

"I need to know why my sister had to die. I understand my fucking father. He was the one who made the deal. He's the one who was responsible."

"Ya, he's the one, but it may just have been bad luck."

"It wasn't. It was the deal. It had to be."

"K, what do you know about his deal?"

Steven looked at his coffee cup. It was empty.

"Not much really."

"When did he make it?"

"He went on a business trip when I was 12. He came back with this guitar." Steven pointed down at the guitar case beside him. Billy looked down at the case.

"Afterward, things changed, got better. We had money."

"When did your dad die?"

"Three months ago. It's been three months since my family died, since my sister died." Steven looked at his coffee cup. It was full.

He looked up at Billy in surprise.

"Ya Frank made a deal to have this joint. In fact, I think there is 6 Ol' Scratch Taverns scattered about with a version of Frank in each. Frank is always going on about his headaches. It must be a bitch to be in 6 places at once."

Steven looked at his full cup of coffee. He took a sip. It was great coffee.

"It's good coffee, isn't it?" Billy raised his cup and took a sip. "It's too bad that it's almost over."

"What do you mean?"

"That's what I was trying to get to. Frank's deal is a standard contract. 6 years, 6 months and 6 days. I don't know fer sure, but I'm pretty sure he's just about done."

"My sister died 6 years, and I think 6 months from when my dad went on his business trip that changed everything."

Billy nodded his head.

"So it was a standard 666 contract. Now you can work out the exact day yer dad was here and went to the crossroads. I don't know that helps much, but it's a start. I don't get the guitar though. Was yer dad, a famous guitar player?"

"No, he never played. He made his money trading."

"Trading?"

"Ya, he managed clients' money for them."

Billy had no idea what Steven was talking about. He sighed, took a swallow of his coffee.

"I'm not going to talk you oudda goin', and I ain't a hypocrite. Take 11 west for 6 miles, then turn south at the turnoff at the gas station. 6 miles exactly, you'll come to the crossroads."

"Thanks," Steven said. Billy stood. "I ain't done you no favours. I should have left ya be, but iffin' yer dad made a deal and that there guitar has sumpin' ta do with it, well shit who knows." Billy turned and left.

Steven finished his coffee and left the Ol' Scratch. He walked out to the blacktop and started walking west. He walked for half an hour without seeing a car. He paused to look at a highway sign. It read '11.'

He continued west, and almost immediately, an old red pickup slowed and pulled up beside him.

"Where ya headed, son?" The face of the driver who peered at him through the open window was a mass of wrinkles. An old dog lay on the blanket that covered the seat.

A SINGLE ROUND

"Morning. Thanks for stopping. I'm just heading up the road a bit to a service station."

"Well, I can take you that far fer sure. That's where I turn. Hop in."

Steven put his guitar in the back along with his backpack. He pulled the door open and climbed into the truck.

The dog sniffed his hand, whimpered, lay its head down on its paws and went back to sleep.

"This here is Gunner."

"Hey, Gunner." Steven patted the old dog.

"Not all dat sure Gunner hears much, but he's a good ol' dog."

Gunner raised his head and looked up at the old man.

The old guy smiled and pushed the truck into gear. The truck rumbled along. The old guy was dressed in jeans and a denim shirt. He had a sweat-stained green ball-cap.

"Name's Allen."

"Steven."

"Where ya headed? Yer not from round here."

"My mother was. She grew up on a farm around here. Family name of Cooper."

"Cooper ya say. Ya, I seem to recollect some folks named Cooper farmed around here but dat was sometime back. I was jus a kid. Seems ta remember some trouble wit 'em."

"Couldn't have been my mother's family. She just passed. She was in her 40's. She left the farm probably in the 80s."

"Don't s'pose."

The fields rolled by. Steven breathed deep. The strong smell of earth filled him. It was good. The sky was clear.

"Crops er coming long nicely. Should be a good year if we git enough rain," Allen said, not really to Steven. Steven looked at the fields, not understanding what the old guy saw but feeling content.

He realized he felt like he was home. As though he had been away for his entire life, and here he was coming home. The air smelled like home somehow. He had never been here, and something inside him quieted. A small thing that had buzzed and fluttered his entire life was quiet for the first time. He only noticed it in its absence.

"Well, here we are. I'm turnin south. It's nun of my bin'nus but would you be head dat way too?"

Steven looked at the old man and his sharp, shrewd eyes. A small grin was playing with his mouth.

"Yeah, I am," Steven said.

"Ha knew it. Yer fixin to see da Judge, ain't cha?" Allen smiled as if he had guessed a great secret.

"Yeah, I am," Steven said quietly.

"Well, it ain't my pig an' it ain't my farm bu' I think yer just batshit crazy!"

Steven laughed. "You may be right."

Allen laughed back. "Well, den I s'pose ah kin drive ya there. It's a might early. Tell ya what, let's head to my farm. My Doreen will fix us some lunch an I'll put ya ta work fer a bit then I'll drive to the crossroads ta do yer bin'nus."

"I don't want to put you out, but that would be great."

Allen slowed and turned south. Steven saw the sign 'township road 78'. The truck bounced and hesitated and rumbled on as Allen shifted through the gears.

Gunner raised his head and sat up. He knew he was almost home. Suddenly the cab of the truck filled with a stink Steven couldn't identify. It was foul.

"Fuck Gunner, couldn't ya waited, jeez!" Allen said and laughed. Steven groaned and laughed as well. They were still laughing when Allen turned the truck off the road and pulled up beside a nice bungalow in a large farmyard. He stopped and shut the truck off in front of a garage with its door open. Past the garage was a large old red hip-roofed barn.

"C'mon."

They walked from the truck, Gunner leading up to the two-tone small pretty house. The wooden stairs had small flower pots with pansies of various colours. It was obvious, Allen and Doreen were proud of their home.

The door opened, and an enormous woman filled the doorway. She had an equally enormous smile on her face.

"Allen, what have you brought home?"

"This here is Steven. He's coming for a spot of lunch, and later I'm driving him over to have a meeting."

She looked down at Gunner, who licked her hand. Gunner lay down on a mat by the door. The woman looked back at Steven and frowned. "Well, I'm happy to feed him fer sure. No good kin come from those meetauns. No how." She stepped back, and Allen held the door for Steven.

"You don't take her no heed. I know nuthin we kin says gonna change yer mind, so that's that. Go on in."

Doreen scowled at Allen; her big smile returned as she guided Steven to the dining room.

"Here, sit here. I'm afraid it's not much. I was making grilled onion and cheese sandwiches."

"That sounds fantastic," Steven said and meant it.

Allen came in and sat in his chair. There was a glass of water in front of him. Doreen called from the kitchen, "Drink yer water, Allen."

Allen grumbled and drank the water. Steven watched him. Allen had been a tall man, now bent over and shrunken. His fingers reminded Steven of day-old chicken wings, dry, brown and shrivelled. The skin over his knuckles was thin and had a papery look; between the knuckles, his skin was very dark, almost black.

Doreen came in and placed plates in front of Steven and Allen with two triangles of toasted bread dripping with cheese and sliced onions. They smelled wonderful. She kissed Allen on his bald head as she passed him. Allen's face was tanned dark from his neckline to just above his nose, and from there up his skin was fish white. He had a few stray white hairs on the top of his head, but mostly he was completely bald.

Doreen came in with a plate for herself.

"What can I get you to drink, Steven?"

"Water would be great thanks."

She left and returned with a glass of water for him.

Steven was about to pick up his sandwich when Doreen grabbed his hand and grasping Allen's hand, she bent her head. Steven looked to Allen, who winked and bowed his head. Steven bowed his head and waited.

After a minute, Doreen raised her head and smiled at Steven. "Dig in."

She picked up her sandwich and ate. Steven followed suit. They didn't talk as they ate. It was a quiet, efficient meal. When they had finished, Doreen picked up the plates and headed back to the kitchen.

"Coffee?" she called over her shoulder.

"I would love a cup, my love," Allen said.

"Yes, that would be great," Steven said.

"Hey, Doreen. You 'member a family that farmed 'round some time back, name of Cooper?"

"What's that? Cooper?" her head came around the corner. "Cooper? Naw don't think so," her head disappeared. She came back around carrying three cups of coffee. She had a puzzled look on her face as she placed the cups in front of Allen and Steven. She took a sip and said, "Oh my word, be forgetting my head next." She rose quickly and came back with a carton of milk and a sugar bowl. She had a furrowed brow and sat back down.

"Unless yer talking 'bout the Coopers over west road 84 by the Peterson farm? But that's way back. I was jus' a girl den." She took a sip of coffee. "I remember my folks talking about it. Hell, most ah da town were jawin' about it. Some bad bizness. A bear attack or sumptin." She looked at Allen.

"Ya, I 'member it too. I was a bit older than you, but it was my brothers that told me 'bout it. Sum said the little girl cut up her folks while they slept. Chopped dem up good and her brother and little sister. My brother said that they had heard that there was even blood on the ceiling. It was everywhere." He paused to take a sip of his coffee. His fingers stabbed the air.

"It weren't that little girl. My pa said she was just a little spit of a thing. No how could she have done the butchery that they said had bin done."

"Course dat was a long time back an can't be nuthin ta do with yer ma."

"Dat yer family name?" Doreen asked.

"Ya. My mother's family. She came from around here."

"Sorry, don't know any Coopers 'round here septin that old story."

"No, that's fine. Whatever happened to the girl?" Steven asked.

"Well, don't rightly know. Seems she disappeared. Jus' up and vanished from the cop shop still covered in blood an all. Never heard 'bout her agin."

After coffee Allen took Steven out to the back, Gunner walked alongside.

"You ever drove a tractor afore?" Allen asked.

"No, sir."

"Well, it ain't hard. I got a job fer ya. It ain't very exciting but needs doin'."

"Sure, anything I can do to help."

Allen climbed up and sat on the metal seat.

"C'mon up."

Steven mimicked Allen grabbing the huge black tire and the top of the tractor. There was a step for his foot. Allen moved to give him room, then started the tractor. It started almost immediately with a roar, and a cloud of black smoke erupted from the exhaust pipe that stood straight up from the center of the tractor. He pointed at a series of three levers, chrome with black knobs. He pointed at the first one.

"Ya don't need ta worry 'bout this one. Just these two. This one is up, and this is down," he called over the engine's noise. He pushed one lever down and attached to the tractor a sort of a flat piece of iron moved down with a deep whine sound. Allen pulled on the next lever and the flat iron moved up. Behind the piece of iron attached with chains to the tractor, was a flat pallet of wood. There were a couple of rocks on the pallet.

"Got it?" He grinned as if he were imparting great difficult knowledge.

"Sure?" Steven said, not really sure. Allen grinned and shut the tractor off. It was suddenly really quiet.

"So like ah said, it ain't excitin' werk. Ya drive 'round this here field, and when ya see a stone, you drive over it and push down on the lever. That drops the picker down, and then you raise it and the rock lands on the float. That's it."

"That's it? Just pick up stones?" said Steven.

Allen started climbing down from the tractor. "Yup, that's it."

"Cool. Ok. I can do that."

"Ok, off you go. I'll flag ya down when it's suppertime."

Steven climbed in the seat of the tractor. The metal seat was surprisingly comfortable. Allen leaned forward. Steven pushed the red 'start' button, and the tractor came to life, spouting a black cloud. Allen nodded and smiled, hands on his hips.

"Oh, ya." He climbed up beside Steven.

"Ah forgot. That there." He pointed to a pedal next to Steven's left foot.

"That there is the clutch an that there," he pointed to the pedal next to Steven's right foot, "is the brake an the throttle is here under the steering wheel." He grabbed a small lever sitting on a half-circle of metal. He pushed the lever to the right, and the engine sped up; the black smoke disappeared.

"You kin leave it there. Seecon gear is going to be fast enough." He looked at Steven skeptically. "You know haw ta drive stick?"

"Yes, sir," Steven said. Steven saw Allen sigh, relieved. He climbed down from the tractor and stepped back. Steven pushed down on the clutch, shifted into what he guessed was first and let the clutch out slowly. The tractor lurched forward, nearly throwing him backward off the seat. He pushed in the clutch.

Allen was grinning with Gunner standing beside him. Steven moved the shifter into his second guess at first gear and let out the clutch. The tractor lurched forward and started to move. Steven grinned at Allen. Allen waved and started walking back to the barn, Gunner, at his side.

It took a few tries to lower the picker enough to catch the stones, but not too far to grab a lot of dirt. But once he got it, he fell easily into a routine. The noise of the tractor faded. He found his mind wandered. He thought of his mom and her stories. So many stories, all of them quaint and otherworldly like her with her quiet elegance. Her soft-spoken ease. He got lost in the past, and it was a surprise when he heard a clanging. At first, he thought he had damaged the tractor; after a second, he looked around and saw Allen standing waving at him with Gunner not far off. Steven turned the tractor, lifted the rock picker and drove to Allen. He shut the tractor off. Steven was shocked at the quiet. He stood. His ass was asleep. He climbed down slowly.

"Ya done good. Betcha, yer butt is on the sore side." Allen laughed.

Together they walked towards the house. It was near sunset. The trees cast long shadows across the yard. Everything had a warm feel. Steven looked about, tired and content.

Gunner came loping from the trees to the north.

They got to the house. Steven noticed the large metal triangle hung by the back door. It had been the clanging he had heard. He smiled at the simplicity of it.

Inside, Doreen said, "Go wash up. Supper's ready."

Steven went into the small washroom. He was shocked at what he saw. His face was covered in grey-black dirt. His eyes nearly glowed out of his face. His lips stood out, pink and wet, and there were streaks running down the sides of his head from sweat. He washed. He had to work at getting the black from his nostrils, mouth and ears.

He tasted the grit. He swished water around his mouth. It took a bit of time, but when he stepped out of the bathroom; he was more or less clean. He walked through the kitchen. It smelled wonderful.

"I thought we'd have a special meal for our guest," Doreen said.

Allen was already seated in his spot. He grinned as Steven walked in.

"Sure glad yer here. Mighta had grilled cheese sandwiches agin."

"I heard that, an you ain't so hard done by."

"No I ain't. Just funnin'. You know dat."

She grinned at him. He looked like a mischievous old gnome.

"We're having roast chicken, fresh potatoes an green beans from the garden. You come by at the perfect time. The garden is puttin' out like you never saw, an I just butchered a few hens last week."

"Oh, boy." Allen leaned forward, childlike.

"That sounds wonderful. It smells amazing," Steven said.

As Doreen headed for the kitchen, she said "Maybe after the dishes are cleared, you kin play us a tune on that there guitar ya got."

Steven stopped smiling. "I wish I could. I don't know how to play. It's not my guitar."

Allen looked up.

"It was my dad's."

"He was a player?" Allen asked.

"No. It's hard to explain."

Allen nodded as Doreen came in with a big roasting pan.

"Allen put down a towel." Allen reached behind him to the cupboard and pulled out a tea towel. He spread it out flat on the table to protect the surface. Doreen put the roasting pan on the cloth. She lifted the lid with a flourish. The roast chicken was browned to perfection, surrounded by potatoes. She smiled with pride and went back to the kitchen. She came back with steamed green beans and a gravy boat.

She sat with a sigh. She looked at the table, looked at Allen with love, and to Steven with kindness. She reached for their hands and hung her head. Steven and Allen bowed with her.

She looked up, smiling.

"Well, let's eat."

She stood and took Steven's plate. She served him some potatoes.

"White or dark? Yer a dark meat kinda guy, aren't you.?" She smiled, and Steven nodded.

She piled his plate with chicken and beans and covered them with gravy. She handed Steven his plate.

"Enjoy."

"That's a lot of food." He smiled.

"Ya werked fer it."

She smiled as she served Allen.

"Thank you, dear," Allen said.

Still smiling she served herself. She sat. Looked at her table and Allen and Steven. She ate. Again they ate in silence efficiently. When they were done, she cleared the dishes. She came back.

"I think the dishes kin wait this evening," she said, almost apologetically.

"How bout a round of Bunco, " she said.

Allen smiled and reached behind him to the cupboard. He pulled out a deck of cards.

Steven had never played Bunco, but he got a handle on it and hours passed. Doreen kept up a steady monologue about crops, old stories and town gossip.

Around 11, she just stopped. She looked up at Steven with sadness in her eyes.

"Is there anything we can say to you to stop you from heading to the crossroads? You seem happy here. Yer a good person and a good worker. Yer welcome to stay here. Our son has long since moved out. You can stay in his room. God knows we could use the help round here."

"Mother," Allen said quietly and touched her arm.

"I know.. I know." There were tears in her eyes."It's just such a waste." She looked at Steven. "That creature has ruined so many lives hereabouts." Angrily, she wiped the tears from her eyes.

She stood.

"It has been a real fine pleasure meeting you, Steven. I hope you find what you are searching for. Now it's time for a foolish old woman to find her bed. Goodbye, Steven." She squeezed his hand and left the room. They watched her go.

Allen looked at Steven, turned in his seat and pulled from the cupboard a mason jar with clear liquid and two shot glasses. He unscrewed the lid and filled the shot glasses. He put the lid on and put the jar back behind him in the cupboard. He pushed one of the glasses to Steven.

Steven hesitated, then reached out and took the glass.

Allen looked at the liquid.

"This here is the finest shine that'll ever touch to yer lips. A fella not far down the road brews it up. Name of Jacob."

"I met Jacob last night at Frank's."

"Ya, I'm not surprised. He's a stand-up guy." Allen paused.

"We should git going." Allen knocked the shot back.

Steven followed suit, bracing himself for the burn. A burn that didn't come. It was as smooth as any fine scotch in his father's liquor cabinet. He felt the warmth slide down his throat.

Allen looked at him, a smile playing on his lips. "Good stuff, Huh?"

"Yes," Steven said. "It's really good."

Allen chuckled.

"Let's go." He stood, and Steven followed as he left the house.

Outside it was dark. Off to the south was a strip of lighter blue, vibrant in the dark. The area in front of the garage was lit by a yardlight that cast deep shadows everywhere. Gunner came walking out from the shadows and climbed into the truck when Allen opened the door. Steven walked around the truck, put his backpack and guitar

A SINGLE ROUND

case in the back and climbed in. The truck whined as they backed up and turned around.

Allen was quiet as they turned out onto 78, heading south. The cool night air came in the open windows. The sky was laced with stars. Steven felt calmer than he had in months. He was nearing his goal, and he felt no nervousness, just a sense of ease and well-being.

He looked out across the fields.

Allen cleared his throat. Steven could see he had something to say and was working up to it.

"Doreen is right. Nuthin good comes from meeting with The Judge an I ain't getting any younger. You would be a great help." He paused. "What she didn't say.. Was...well we had a son. He's gone. He's never coming back." Allen slowed the truck. Gunner watched him. He stopped and turned to look at Steven.

"He met with the Judge, and 6 years later he was gone. I never found out why..." Allen lapsed into silence. He pushed the truck into gear and started moving. "Just think about it. You can werk the farm and who knows one day it could be yers. It's a good farm. Bin good to me and mine." Allen didn't look at Steven.

"I'm not going to make a deal. I need to ask a question. That's it. I need to know why he killed my sister. That's it. I just need to know. And return his cursed guitar."

Allen didn't say anything. They drove in silence, staring ahead at the two yellowy puddles that led them down the road. Allen turned off the road and swung the truck around, stopping in the middle of the road.

"This is it." He checked the clock on the dash. It was almost midnight.

"Thank you for everything. I'm sorry about your son. I have to do this."

Allen looked straight ahead. He seemed not to hear. Steven got out of the truck and pulled his backpack and guitar from the back. He stood and looked at Allen. Allen looked at him.

"It was fine, meetin ya."

He completed his U-turn, and Steven watched as the weak tail lights faded into the dark as the truck rattled away. It became quiet. Very quiet. Steven put his pack and guitar case down. The cool air carried the smell of earth, the sweet smell of growing crops, and water. A breeze stirred the grass along the side of the road.

Steven stood in the center of the crossroads. He looked down the road in each of the four directions. No lights could be seen on the road in any direction.

He jumped when behind him, an engine revved loudly. He spun 'round and found a car stopped inches from his legs.

It was black and very shiny. Steven knew a bit about cars. Enough to recognize a '69 GTO. He chuckled to himself. Of course, the 69 GTO was often called The Goat. There was even a model called The Judge. It made sense.

The driver's door opened, and a man slid out. He was tall and dressed in a fine suit. He had a smile you could blind yourself looking at. Steven had seen that kind of smile before. His father had a smile like that, it never touched his eyes. This man's smile did not touch his eyes either. His eyes were dark and hard.

The Judge walked around his car, easy and supremely in his element.

"Howdy. Steven, isn't it?"

"Yes, my name is Steven. I brought you something."

"For me. How unusual. What is it?"

"It's the guitar you gave my father."

"Your father, really." He bent and opened the guitar case.

"My, my, this is one fine guitar." he pulled the guitar from the case. "This is a Kalamazooo KG-14 flat-top. You don't see those every day for sure." He held it with reverence. "But son, I never gave this to your dad."

He returned the guitar to its case but left it open. He stood looking down at the guitar. When he looked up, Steven held a chrome long barrel .45 pointed at his head. The Judge smiled.

"You seem to be upset."

A SINGLE ROUND

"Why'd you have to kill my sister?"

"Your sister? Son..."

"Stop calling me son I'm not your son." The gun was shaking in Steven's hand.

The Judge smiled.

"I never understand how anyone can think one of your weapons could possibly hurt me. I have been shot, stabbed, blown up and burned. I can't be hurt by...wait, what is..?"

The world exploded in light and noise. Steven turned to see what was happening and tripped, falling backwards. It saved his life. The semi-truck screamed past him, ramming into the Judge, then into the Judges' car. The noise was all-encompassing. The roar filled the world. The truck pushed what was left of the car and the Judge down the road and into the ditch.

Steven picked himself up from the road. It had been close, mere inches. He walked to the wreck.

The Judge stepped out of the ditch, brushing dirt from his lapel. He smiled at Steven.

They both looked up when the door to the ruined cab opened and a man stepped out. It was Gordon. He was bleeding heavily from a gash in his scalp. He fell from the cab onto the grass in the ditch.

"YOU!" Gordon screamed. "YOU! You can't have him." Gordon had managed to stand and was walking slowly toward Steven and the Judge. "You can't have him. Not till I get what you promised."

"But Gordon, that's not the deal."

"You didn't give me what I wanted. I never got what I asked for."

"Oh, Gordon, I think you did. You wanted to be free. You had some romantic notion about truck drivers. You wanted to drive a truck."

"Not forever!"

"Well, yes, however, you never specified for how long you wanted to be 'free' and really, it hasn't been forever. It's only been some 40 years." The Judge smiled. Gordon swayed, slumped to the blacktop. Steven ran to him.

"Hmmm. Looks like we are going to have a visit from Mr. White," the Judge said.

Gordon was sitting propped on one arm. He was bleeding badly. He looked at Steven, scowled, and looked at the Judge.

"You've got him. Now release me. I've driven for you long enough." Gordon said quietly.

"Now, Gordon. That's hardly fair. You got exactly what you asked for. You will continue to drive for me until I say otherwise. That's our deal."

"What did you say?" Steven asked Gordon. Gordon just looked at him, then back to the Judge. "What's he talking about?" Steven asked the Judge.

The Judge frowned. "Well, I sent him to pick you up, but instead, he just had to stop at Frank's. He just can't resist stopping at The Ol' Scratch. I tried to get Billy to drive you over, but Billy has become a bit difficult, listening to Jacob and his 'Jurors'." He made little air quotes with one hand. "So I got Allen to bring you here," the Judge said, finally.

Steven looked at the Judge, "Wait, Allen is marked?" he asked confused.

"Oh Yeah. Both Allen and Doreen are."

"They were so against me coming here. Something to do with their son."

The Judge studied Steven for a minute, he said. "Yeah, they were upset about their son. His deal ran its course. They came to me, demanding I bring him back. So we made a deal."

"You brought their son back. You can do that?" Steven stepped forward.

"Well, yes and no. I can plunk the soul back into their body. It's usually short and extremely painful, but their son had been cremated. No body, so I arranged for Gunner to have an accident and dropped their son into the dog's body. Of course, they're convinced

A SINGLE ROUND

I didn't hold up my end of the deal. Sad, really. Their son is right there." He paused and looked around. "Well shit," he said quietly. Steven followed his gaze.

At the side of the road the remains of the guitar and case lay, a pile of shattered splinters. The Judge walked over to where the pieces rest. He reached down and picked up the guitar, whole and undamaged. He held it before himself admiringly. He turned it back and forth.

"There is something about this guitar. I know this guitar. Ol' Tom gave it to that fine young boy many years ago."

"Who's Ol' Tom?"

"Oh, no one." He glanced quickly at Steven, then back to the guitar. "Your dad must have had deep pockets."

He looked at Steven, holding the beautiful guitar.

"Now, Steven. About your situation. I'm sorry, but I never met your dad. If I had, I certainly would not have given him this guitar."

"LIAR!" Steven screamed and raised the gun.

"Yes, I am a liar, however, not in this instance. I never met with your father, and I never made a deal with him." He smiled and straightened his already straight tie.

"I did meet with your mother, though."

The gun dropped with Steven's arm as it fell to his side.

"My mother?" he asked.

"Oh, yes. It was many years ago. She wanted to be free of her father. He wasn't a nice man. Quite abusive toward her and her little sister. Almost a monster, really. It was just shortly after I had arrived in this neck of the woods."

The Judge paused and looked at the guitar in his hand, then casually he tossed it. The ghost of the guitar vanished before it could hit the ground. The Judge looked down. Beside him on the pavement was the shattered guitar. Absently he said, "I can't fix this. It never entered my realm. Pity." He looked up at Steven. Behind the Judge, Steven noticed the 69 GTO stood whole and undamaged.

"Ah, I see Gordon has crossed over. I'll have to get him a new rig." The Judge smiled.

Steven looked to where Gordon lay. He wasn't breathing.

"Yes, I gave your mother what she wanted. She was quite a woman. She wanted two things. I usually don't go for that sort of contract, but like I said, I was new to the area. We came to an agreement." He smiled. Not his big shit-eating grin but a smaller, almost sheepish grin.

"I may have been a bit too enthusiastic with my efforts to help her."

"The bear attack?"

"Bear? Yes, well, it wasn't a bear. I released a hellhound. They can be messy," he looked out across the dark fields.

"Then I pushed your mom forward in time a bit until the excitement died down around her, and I gave her the second part of her contract."

Steven took a step backward.

"Ah, you have a sense of it. Yes, Steven. I gave her, you. She wanted a son, so I gave her my own."

"No," Steven said. "No."

"Haven't you noticed you are a bit different? How people seem to get hurt around you? It's in your nature."

"No."

"You are my son, Steven, and I have such great hopes for you."

Steven looked at this man in front of him and knew it was true. People had always gotten hurt around him. The more he loved them, the more they got hurt. He cried then. He had loved his little sister so much.

"NO!" He screamed and brought the gun he still held in his hand up to his chin and pulled the trigger.

The report was massive. The sound exploded out, a physical wave carried past the Judge into the night.

Steven never heard the crack of the .45 round. Never heard it echo over the fields. The round tore through Steven's face and head, ripping it to shreds, scattering blood, bone, and brain into the night air. It snapped what was left of his head backward. It tossed his body up and back. Steven's body landed several feet away on the pavement with a wet crunch.

The Judge picked up the gun and walked over to where what was left of Steven lay. He looked down at him for a time. He looked up at the sky with its millions of stars. Off to the west, he noticed the yard light of a farm. To the east, just over the horizon, he could see the soft glow of the far-off city. He looked back to Steven as he lay on the hard blacktop.

"The young are so impulsive. You have to love their passion and spontaneity." He looked at the heavy chrome gun in his hand.

"You will find that you are very hard to kill."
Steven's face began to reform itself. His ripped flesh knitting itself. Jawbone growing, stretching to meet the front part of his skull. Muscle and skin stretched across the newly formed bone. It only took a minute. Steven shifted, coughed, and new eyelids opened. He looked confused, laying on his back, his eyes darted around. He sat bolt upright.

"Wait! What the fuck is going on?"

The Judge walked closer to Steven and extended his hand.

"I told you, you are my son." He helped Steven to his feet. "And I have so many plans for us." He slid his arm around Steven. "Come on, let's go. Hey, you want to drive?"

R A JACOBSON

So tallwalker. Yer done Yessir Yesir,
dats it
Hopin' you lik'd it ver good.
Peck 'er to leave a rear view
Ver fine

A SINGLE ROUND

About the Author

After leaving the Northern forest and farmland of Saskatchewan, Rick headed to Calgary and the Alberta College of Art. After four years of hard work, he came out confused and somewhat lost. Now what?

Rick has been a bounce (one week), a radio switcher (one night), he worked at the CBC (one month). He was a stuntman (two action movies that he never saw, but he's not alone in that) and he modelled briefly (he was the Jolly Green Giant for a time). Rick has built houses, packed groceries, cut grass and has written four and illustrated nineteen children's books. He has worked as a painter, a designer, an illustrator and a writer.

Rick has won awards for his work in advertising and publishing, including the Ruth Schwartz Award, the Amelia Frances Howard-Gibbon Award and numerous national and international awards including the Toronto Art Directors' Awards, Communication Arts Magazine's Award of Excellence, American Illustration Award of Excellence, and the New York Art Directors' Award of Excellence. He has been featured in Smithsonian Magazine, Applied Arts Magazine and in The Artist's Magazine. His commissioned portraits include Robertson Davies, Margaret Atwood, Christopher Ondaatje, and David Thomson.

Rick is currently working on his novel HARD PLACE, and a graphic novel of the same title, to be released in 2021.
Another collection of short stories, A Lead Pill will be released early in 2021.
For Hard Place updates, sign up at deadcatstud.io

R A JACOBSON

Acknowledgments

It sometimes feels like I sold my soul to produce this collection, the novel and graphic novel. The world that these stories and characters spring from consumes me, exerting an increasingly tighter grip.
    I often feel utterly overwhelmed and staggered by the ever-changing and ever-growing list of things I realize I need to do.
    It is also fair to say that it would have never happened without the support and help of my friends and family.
    Sunny listened, read, corrected and listened some more.
    Dave was untiring when I needed an editor or just someone to bounce an idea off. I'm sure I left bruises.
    Jeff gave me access to his vast knowledge of sound and editing.
    Noah stepped up and added his prodigious wordsmithing abilities, and also laid down some perfectly spectacular guitar tracks to accompany the audio version.
    Maite coached me brilliantly as I struggled to find a voice to lend to the characters I had released onto the page.
Mercedes became my first beta reader and forged through what must have been a trial of fire.

Thank you for all the love and support.
Sunniva Foley
Dave Knox
Jeff Bessner
Noah Zacharin
Mike Jacobson
Maite Jacobson
Mercedes Jacobson
Laura Fernandez

A SINGLE ROUND

Other books by R A Jacobson

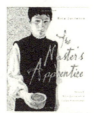

Zombies were people too: The ABZ's of zombies by Rick Jacobson , Sunniva Foley

Ever wonder how a zombie became a zombie. What tragic event fell upon them that turned them into one of the walking dead. In 'Zombies were people too', we find the stories of 26 sad individuals and their untimely demise. With each letter, we are introduced to another tale of zombification. Grab a copy for yourself or anyone who loves a chuckle and zombies. Who doesn't love a good zombie story? Other Formats: Paperback

Click here

The Mona Lisa Caper is based on true events that began to unfold on Monday, August 21, 1911, when Vincenzo Perugia shocked the world by stealing the most famous of the many treasures in the Louvre.

Throughout Rick Jacobson's lively text, Mona Lisa herself narrates the story of her trip back to the city of her creation. The playful art Rick has painted along with his wife, Laura Fernandez, heightens the fun. Not only is it Keystone-Cops funny, it is a sound introduction to the painting that continues to delight, amaze, and mystify hundreds of years after Leonardo da Vinci's death

Click here.

When Marco is sent into apprenticeship with the young master, Michelangelo Buonarroti, much rides on his success. His father has worked very hard as a chemist so that Marco can have a better life, and the boy simply cannot let his family down. Armed with good advice, but more importantly, secret color formulas that his father has taught him, the boy has a good chance at success.

But then he meets the jealous senior apprentice Ridolfo, and before Marco knows it, he has been tricked into looking like a fool. Time and again, the older boy trips him up, until Marco is certain he will be sent home in disgrace.

Click here

Modern art has a language, and when it is learned it opens the door to a lifetime of enjoyment and appreciation. In Picasso: Soul on Fire, Rick Jacobson and Laura Fernandez present more than the story of the painter's life. By exploring his influences and his creative process, they give young readers the tools with which to understand his work.

Click here

'A Single Round' will be released October 24, 2020 and will be available for free for a limited time. Sign up to be notified.

Click here

'A Single Round' the audiobook will be released October 30, 2020 and will be available where ever you get your audiobooks. Sign up to be notified.

Click here

'HARD PLACE' will be released October, 2021 and will be available for free for a limited time. Sign up to be notified.

Click here

'A Lead Pill' will be released January, 2021 and will be available for free for a limited time. Sign up to be notified.

Click here

R A JACOBSON

Hello Shelby, all the Best to you!

Mr. Savu '21

Made in the USA
Monee, IL
07 June 2021